Samuel French Acting E

Those the River Keeps

by David Rabe

SAMUELFRENCH.COM   SAMUELFRENCH.CO.UK

Copyright © 1994 by Ralako, Inc.
All Rights Reserved

THOSE THE RIVER KEEPS is fully protected under the copyright
laws of the United States of America, the British Commonwealth,
including Canada, and all other countries of the Copyright Union. All
rights, including professional and amateur stage productions, recitation,
lecturing, public reading, motion picture, radio broadcasting, television
and the rights of translation into foreign languages are strictly reserved.

ISBN 978-0-573-69469-1

www.SamuelFrench.com
www.SamuelFrench.co.uk

FOR PRODUCTION ENQUIRIES

UNITED STATES AND CANADA
Info@SamuelFrench.com
1-866-598-8449

UNITED KINGDOM AND EUROPE
Plays@SamuelFrench.co.uk
020-7255-4302

Each title is subject to availability from Samuel French, depending
upon country of performance. Please be aware that *THOSE THE
RIVER KEEPS* may not be licensed by Samuel French in your territory.
Professional and amateur producers should contact the nearest Samuel
French office or licensing partner to verify availability.

CAUTION: Professional and amateur producers are hereby warned that
THOSE THE RIVER KEEPS is subject to a licensing fee. Publication of
this play(s) does not imply availability for performance. Both amateurs
and professionals considering a production are strongly advised to apply
to Samuel French before starting rehearsals, advertising, or booking a
theatre. A licensing fee must be paid whether the title(s) is presented for
charity or gain and whether or not admission is charged. Professional/
Stock licensing fees are quoted upon application to Samuel French.

No one shall make any changes in this title(s) for the purpose of
production. No part of this book may be reproduced, stored in a retrieval
system, or transmitted in any form, by any means, now known or yet to
be invented, including mechanical, electronic, photocopying, recording,
videotaping, or otherwise, without the prior written permission of the
publisher. No one shall upload this title(s), or part of this title(s), to any
social media websites.

For all enquiries regarding motion picture, television, and other media
rights, please contact Samuel French.

MUSIC USE NOTE

Licensees are solely responsible for obtaining formal written permission from copyright owners to use copyrighted music in the performance of this play and are strongly cautioned to do so. If no such permission is obtained by the licensee, then the licensee must use only original music that the licensee owns and controls. Licensees are solely responsible and liable for all music clearances and shall indemnify the copyright owners of the play(s) and their licensing agent, Samuel French, against any costs, expenses, losses and liabilities arising from the use of music by licensees. Please contact the appropriate music licensing authority in your territory for the rights to any incidental music.

IMPORTANT BILLING AND CREDIT REQUIREMENTS

If you have obtained performance rights to this title, please refer to your licensing agreement for important billing and credit requirements.

THOSE THE RIVER KEEPS was first produced at the McCarter Theater in Princeton, New Jersey. The cast was as follows:

SUSIE.. Marcia Gay Hardin
PHIL... Anthony LaPaglia
SAL... Burt Young
JANICE ....Debra Cole

THOSE THE RIVER KEEPS was subsequently produced at the American Repertory Company in Cambridge, Massachusetts. The cast was as follows:

SUSIE.. Rebecca Tilney
PHIL.. Paul Guilfoyle
SAL...Jack Willis
JANICE .... Candy Buckley

THOSE THE RIVER KEEPS opened in New York (produced by James B. Freydberg, Kenneth Feld, and Dori Berinstein) at the Promenade Theatre with the following cast:

SUSIE.. Annabella Sciorra
PHIL.. Paul Guilfoyle
SAL... Jude Ciccolella
JANICE ....Phyllis Lyons

All three productions had sets designed by Loren Sherman and were directed by David Rabe.

CHARACTERS

SUSIE
PHIL
SAL
JANICE

TIME

ACT I
Scene 1: a while ago
Scene 2: later
Scene 3: that night

ACT II
Scene 1: three days later
Scene 2: that night

For Jill

ACT I

Scene One

(Phil and Susie's rented house in the Hollywood Hills. The front door is located on the back wall, stage right. The door opens onto a one-step ramp, which runs toward stage left. A picture window is the dominant shape in this back wall. The bedroom door, which is stage left of the window, has a full-length mirror on it facing into the living room. A built-in shelf unit runs along the back wall below the window. The shelf is wide enough and sturdy enough to be sat on, or for someone to lie down on. Downstage left is a small kitchen: refrigerator, sink, small table, some built-in shelves, and a large window. In the wall between the bedroom and the kitchen there is a small closet, its door next to the bedroom door. When it is open, it shows hooks and hangers with Susie's clothing. A box of Pampers. A silver ice bucket stands atop the refrigerator. The living room is on a lower level – though the ramp is only one step – and in it are a couch and coffee table, and a swivel chair located near the step up into the kitchen. Above the swivel chair is a small table with a lamp, a telephone, and an answering machine. Against the downstage right wall is a wooden cabinet. Not in any way immediately apparent is the fact that it is a liquor cabinet. A record player sits nearby with a photo of a young woman

*beside it. Above it, a print of birds hangs.
On the cabinet stands a green statue of a
swan. Just upstage of the cabinet, and facing
downstage, is another door, which opens into
a small closet. On the downstage right is a
closet door.)*

(Music, and as the lights come up on the
late afternoon,* **SUSIE** *is discovered with a
thermometer in her mouth.* **SUSIE** *is in her
early thirties and attractive, sexy. Stockings.
No shoes. On her lap is a teddy bear who
is wearing a Pamper. She is just finishing
putting on the Pamper, and as the music
plays, she rocks with the bear, sort of dancing.
Taking the thermometer out of her mouth she
looks at it unhappily, shakes it, and puts
it back into her mouth. She is startled by a
rattle at the door. As the door opens and the
music ends, she struggles to hide the bear,
holding it behind her back.* **PHIL** *enters. He's
rugged, late forties, dressed in dark slacks,
a blue T-shirt, and linen shirt. He carries a
brown jacket and three paperback books.)*

PHIL. Hey, Susie.

SUSIE. Hi. Hi.

PHIL. Hi. How you doin'?

SUSIE. I'm okay.

> *(Running to him.)*

PHIL. Great.

> *(She kisses him long and hard. And as his
> hands move around her, trying to extend the
> kiss, she fears he will touch the bear and she*

---

*A license to produce *Those the River Keeps* does not include a
performance license for any third-party or copyrighted music. Licensees
should create an original composition or use music in the public domain.
For further information, please see Music Use Note on page 3.

pulls back and he looks at her as she backs away.)

Whatsamatter?

SUSIE. Nothin'. Whata you mean? I'm great.

(She moves to couch for her jacket, which she uses to conceal the bear.)

PHIL. Good. You goin' somewhere?

SUSIE. Dinner, okay?

PHIL. Sure. Where you goin'?

SUSIE. With Janice. She's got somethin' to talk to me about.

PHIL. What?

SUSIE. I don't know.

(She settles on the couch and, taking up her purse, starts tending to her lipstick. The bear, covered by the coat, is in the corner of the couch.)

PHIL. Some guy, right? Another one of those surfer assholes, right?

SUSIE. Maybe.

PHIL. What does she see in those guys?

SUSIE. I don't know. How was your day?

PHIL. It was terrific. I'm very close, I think. I gave a very good audition, which I would say, I don't think this guy was expecting.

(As he is about to join her on the couch she jumps up.)

SUSIE. You want a beer?

PHIL. Yeah, great.

*(**SUSIE** moves toward the kitchen, **PHIL** following along. She gets him a beer and sets it on the kitchen table, where he settles.)*

So he was caught off guard, and also, I think in general he liked me. He talked to me a very long time. He didn't have to do that – because he's a big deal, this guy, in television, and he was askin' me all these questions, you know, personal questions which I took it to be his desire to somehow determine if I had some personal connection to the character, from my background, my life.

SUSIE. Great.

> *(She heads back toward the bear and jacket on the couch.)*

PHIL. He even mentioned these books, which I got the feeling he felt I should read them. So I bought 'em. I feel certain I'm going to get a callback.

SUSIE. Great.

PHIL. What is the matter with you?

SUSIE. Nothing. What do you mean? I'm just in a hurry.

> *(She rushes to the fridge.)*

PHIL. You got this manner. You know, you got this manner.

SUSIE. *(She takes a plate of cold cuts out of the fridge.)* I don't know what you're talking about, I swear I don't. Here's a little dinner. Sorry it's not more.

PHIL. You're givin' me the goddamn heebie-jeebies with this manner – could you stop it?

SUSIE. *(She moves for the bear on the couch and picks it up, conceals it.)* Some guy was by before. He wanted to see you.

PHIL. What guy?

SUSIE. You weren't here. I told him you'd be back.

> *(She starts for the bedroom.)*

PHIL. Wait a minute, I wanna know about this.

> *(He rises and blocks her before she can get into the bedroom.)*

What guy? What'd he look like?

SUSIE. I don't know.

PHIL. How can you not know what he looked like?

SUSIE. He was just this guy.

*(She doesn't know where to go with the bear
now, where to hide it. She heads for the closet.)*

PHIL. You saw him, he was here. What, did fuckin' amnesia
set in?

SUSIE. No.

PHIL. So, what'd he look like?

SUSIE. He was some guy, Phil.

PHIL. Did he have clothes on?

SUSIE. He looked like you.

PHIL. He don't look like me. I'm me. How could he look like
me? This is hostile, Susie. You are really pissed at me.
You are fucking crazy how you are pissed at me.

*(By now she has managed to stuff the bear
into an oversized purse and has put on her
coat. She walks to the couch to pick up the car
keys from off the coffee table.)*

SUSIE. I gotta go.

PHIL. No you don't. Straightening this out is what you gotta
do.

SUSIE. Anyway, you're the one who's hostile, givin' me this
goddamn third degree about this guy.

PHIL. What third degree?

SUSIE. You're drivin' me crazy about this guy, Phil.

PHIL. But you saw him. He come to the door. You talked
to him. But when I wanna know one simple thing, like
what did he look like, you start acting totally imposed
upon. Help me out here.

SUSIE. He knew you.

PHIL. I know a lotta people.

SUSIE. He was from your past.

*(As she opens the door to go, he stops her,
grabbing the door.)*

PHIL. Did he say that?

SUSIE. Yeh.

PHIL. What'd he say?

SUSIE. He didn't say it. It wasn't that he said it.

PHIL. You just said he said it. Did he or didn't he?

SUSIE. He communicated it.

PHIL. Which I wouldn't mind a little of in this conversation here, okay? I don't know what you're talkin' about!

SUSIE. His manner. It was in his manner. It was in his manner he was obviously from your past.

PHIL. *(Crosses to the picture window, parts the blinds with his fingers to peek out.)* What about it?

SUSIE. Your manner, Phil. You have a manner. Nobody else around here has this same manner. This is California. People are not like you here, normally. This guy was like that. So you get it now?

PHIL. Yeh.

> *(Still looking out the window.)*

SUSIE. You know who he was?

PHIL. No. Did he say anything whatsoever, it might be taken as a hint of what he wanted?

SUSIE. No. Did you get to the bank? I need some cash.

PHIL. What about your credit cards? We went through all the aggravation to get them, where are they? Use them.

> *(He grabs the purse and starts looking for the credit cards.)*

Why don't you use them?! I mean, we –

> *(He pulls the bear from the bag and stands, gaping at it.)*

Ohhhhhhh...! Susie, Ohhhhh, look at this. Don't go out, okay. Ohhhh, you're startin' to do this diaper stuff with the bear again. I didn't realize you were so upset. Look how upset you are. This is horrible. This is terrible, Susie.

SUSIE. *(Embarrassed, she sinks onto the couch.)* I did it when I was little and I do it now.

PHIL. *(Moving to her.)* I mean, look at this pathetic little guy, though. This is heartbreaking, Susie.

SUSIE. Look, Phil, havin' a kid is a very large responsibility, and if you're not ready for it, nobody can make you ready for it, so let's just drop it, okay.

(As he joins her on the couch.)

PHIL. All I was sayin' last night was maybe I didn't want a kid right now – right this second. That's what I was sayin'.

SUSIE. But to wake me up in the middle of the night like that.

PHIL. I was worried.

SUSIE. But to just wake me up like that and I'm half-asleep and I'm so vulnerable. I don't know if I'm awake or not and you just say you don't want to have a baby, it just goes into my heart like a knife.

(She takes the bear back.)

PHIL. I was feelin' funny, you know, itchy, that's why I did it.

SUSIE. Why did you do it?

PHIL. I wanted you to know.

SUSIE. I mean why did you really wake me up and say it like that?

PHIL. I wanted you to know.

SUSIE. You don't even know why, you just did it.

PHIL. I wanted you to know. I can't sleep. I'm up half the night floppin' around in the bed like a goddamn fish!

SUSIE. What I think maybe is you're tryin' to tell me the bottom line is that you really don't wanna have a kid ever – and this is all some kind of code – that you are like totally opposed, and that is what you're really sayin'. Really.

*(As **PHIL** is leaning in to gently kiss her.)*

PHIL. No, no.

SUSIE. Janice says I should divorce you.

PHIL. What? She says what?

SUSIE. I told her. She was really pissed off, boy, she –

PHIL. What's she gotta be mad about? What business is it of hers?

> *(Leaping up, he heads to the kitchen and grabs a beer.)*

Fuck her.

SUSIE. She's my friend. She loves me. She's just tryin' to look out for my well-being. There's nothin' wrong with that.

PHIL. The hell with her. She hates me.

> *(Crossing to the picture window to nervously peek out.)*

SUSIE. Oh, it doesn't matter anyway. Because, you know, it's over for me this month anyway.

PHIL. What's over?

SUSIE. I mean, I ovulated, Phil, that's what I think. I mean, today is early but –

PHIL. When? You did?

> *(He moves back to her now, wants to keep her on the couch.)*

SUSIE. So you don't have to worry about it. I mean, we have a whole month now to figure this mess out, aren't we lucky.

PHIL. Come home early then. Don't go out.

SUSIE. I gotta. She's waitin'.

PHIL. Stay home.

> *(Kissing her neck, her cheek.)*

Don't go see that damn Janice, Susie.

SUSIE. I'm gonna be late the way it is.

PHIL. You gonna take the car?

SUSIE. Of course I'm gonna take the car. I told you.

PHIL. What am I gonna do?

SUSIE. What were you gonna do? Were you gonna go out?

PHIL. I don't know. I just got home.

>*(He pulls her toward the couch and they sprawl over the arm, **SUSIE** on top of him. The phone rings. Kiss. The phone rings, and the machine picks up.)*

VOICE OF JANICE. Susie! Hi! Where are you? It's me. I got here a little early, but you should be here by now. Susie?

>*(**SUSIE** pulls back from **PHIL**.)*

Are you there, Hon? We really have to talk. I mean, I think what you said is really something we have to take seriously.

>*(**SUSIE** leaps to her feet.)*

SUSIE. Oh, God, she's gonna kill me.

PHIL. Who cares? C'mon!

SUSIE. I gotta! I gotta.

>*(She bends, gives him a quick kiss, and runs out the door.)*

PHIL. Come home early! Okay?

>*(He is sprawled there. **JANICE** is still going on, and he turns, glares at the source of her voice, the machine.)*

VOICE OF JANICE. I mean, I just can't stop thinking about your situation. I'm really eager to talk to you. I guess you're on your way. I hope so. If you're not, and you get this, I'm at –

PHIL. *(Storming over to the machine.)* Janice, whata you gotta BUST MY BALLS!

>*(He grabs the phone up.)*

I'M BEGGIN' YOU! GET OUTA MY LIFE!

>*(He listens.)*

No. She's gone. No.

(Slamming the phone down, he sees the teddy bear on the couch.)

PHIL. And you... You silly...motherfucker...!

(He puts it in the swivel chair and covers it with the blanket.)

Go to sleep.

(As he presses down on the blanket, perhaps a little too hard, the music* starts. Weird yet lush, spooky. He stands for a second, worried, then looks to the window, goes up to the window. He peers out, turning and facing downstage as the lights go out.)

(Blackout.)

---

*A license to produce *Those the River Keeps* does not include a performance license for any third-party or copyrighted music. Licensees should create an original composition or use music in the public domain. For further information, please see Music Use Note on page 3.

Scene Two

(*The music* plays in the blackout and then the refrigerator light comes on, the door already open. A dark silhouette of a man against the light facing into the cold blue glow of the interior. Other lights rise to show* **PHIL** *asleep on the couch. The figure at the refrigerator lights a Zippo lighter. The music cuts out and the lights come up on Phil and Susie's apartment,* **PHIL** *crying out and waking up and leaping to his feet to face* **SAL**, *who stands in the kitchen, lighting a cigarette.* **SAL** *is dressed in a dark suit with a faint pinstripe, shiny dark shoes, a fancy tie, a pinky ring.*)

PHIL. That was you. You were here before.

SAL. I was lookin' for you. I was wonderin' how you are.

PHIL. How'd you find me?

SAL. Phil, I can find anybody. And you ain't exactly hidden.

PHIL. No.

SAL. So what's up?

PHIL. You're askin' me?

SAL. Yeh.

PHIL. I'm just livin' my life, you know.

SAL. So how's it goin'?

PHIL. Not bad.

SAL. That's good.

PHIL. Whata you, a fuckin' social worker, Sal? Huh? Is this a situation, here? Do I have to be calculatin' the pros and cons of do-I-need-precautionary measures, or not?

SAL. Whata you mean?

---

*A license to produce *Those the River Keeps* does not include a performance license for any third-party or copyrighted music. Licensees should create an original composition or use music in the public domain. For further information, please see Music Use Note on page 3.

PHIL. You haven't changed your line of work, I don't think.

SAL. I like my work.

PHIL. So that's my point.

SAL. You ain't in trouble with anybody, are you? I hope not.

PHIL. I ain't. I mean, currently.

SAL. So the past is the past.

PHIL. Right. Except some people got long memories. We both know this.

SAL. I certainly do.

> (**SAL** *starts to prowl around the house, moving upstage along the ramp, glancing in the closet, the bedroom door.*)

PHIL. As do I. So that's what I'm sayin'. You're here. Like there's some flying saucer, it has dropped you off. This time machine. Right. What is goin' on here? My past history is like this fuckin' cloud, right, and anything could step out of it. I did. You see what I'm sayin' to you, Sal – I don't know why you're here.

SAL. I missed you.

PHIL. Right, and besides that.

SAL. Gimme a drink. Whata you got to drink?

PHIL. Since when have you started to drink, Sal? You never used to drink.

> (**PHIL** *moves to the bar, a low cabinet against the stage right wall, keeping distance between himself and* **SAL**.)

SAL. That's right. I didn't used to. But are we frozen in time, Phil? I don't think so.

PHIL. But it was a point with you. "I am Sal. I don't drink."

SAL. Stress. I have a lot of stress in my life. Career-related stress.

PHIL. So stress has caused you to start drinking?

SAL. But only in moderation, and I don't take no fuckin' pills – I know a lotta guys, they take these pills.

PHIL. So what's botherin' you?

SAL. It's been a gradual thing – so I went to this fortune-teller. Fuck her. She was no help whatsoever.

(Having prowled to the front door, **SAL** *moves along the window.)*

PHIL. What's she say?

SAL. Bourbon. You got bourbon? You're a class guy.

(He steps into the bedroom.)

PHIL. Sure.

(Takes bourbon and glass out of liquor cabinet.)

This is exciting. You come by. You want a drink. You're different.

SAL. *(Stepping out of the bedroom.)* I ain't that different.

PHIL. So what'd this fortune teller say?

SAL. She says bullshit. Death is what she wants to talk about. I tole her to fuck off.

(Seeing that **PHIL** *has the liquor out,* **SAL** *heads to the kitchen and the refrigerator to get the ice.)*

PHIL. Sal, Sal, I think she coulda been on to somethin' there. Death could be stress-related.

SAL. *(Taking the ice bucket from on top of the refrigerator, he fills it.)* You think I made a mistake? Maybe I did. Maybe I should call her up – apologize – whata you think? Tell her if her thought hasn't been lost and she can scrounge it up outa the fuckin' outer space, or wherever the hell she gets it in the first place, I'll fly back, I wanna know. My friend Phil who has been lost will come back with me – we both want to know – we both are hungry as little babies to know...

(Crossing with the ice toward **PHIL**, *who waits at the coffee table.)*

...what was her point in saying to me, "Death is imminent."

PHIL. You didn't say that. That was what she said?

SAL. I told you.

PHIL. No, no, no.

> *(Taking the ice bucket, he sits on the couch, preparing to make the drinks.)*

You tole me the one part, but you left out the other part. You tole me the death part, but you left out the imminent part.

SAL. Now this is very important. I want the bourbon in the exact manner that I am going to describe. First, three ice cubes. One, two, three.

PHIL. Three ice cubes?

SAL. That's right. Not two, not four. Three. Then the two shots perfectly measured, they are poured onto the ice, which is then allowed to melt into the bourbon for twelve seconds. Not ten, not fourteen, but twelve. At which point, the third shot is poured and a final ice cube.

> *(This has all been done, **SAL** signaling **PHIL** to pour the final shot. **SAL** drops in the final ice cube.)*

PHIL. So this works for your stress? I mean, you're satisfied with the results?

SAL. Up to a point.

PHIL. *(Pouring his own drink.)* Right. What more is there? There's this point and that point – which brings me to the point I was trying to make a bit ago, I don't know if I did or didn't.

SAL. So what was it?

PHIL. Well, history. Right. History. There's yours, there's mine, there's the world's. The universe. Right? The fuckin' universe has got a history. Or so they would have us think.

SAL. I think it does.

PHIL. But what is it? Right? This stuff, you did it, it's gone. That's your history. And so, I agree with that, and speaking personally, my history is like this cloud which is behind me –

SAL. You mentioned that.

PHIL. *(Pacing up near the window.)* It's this cloud, anybody could step out of it and tell me I did anything whatsoever, I would have to agree with them, because I done a great deal. Somebody says, there is this guy, he has a grudge against you, because you insulted his brother in the street outside such and such, they have not forgotten about it. They have tried to forget about it, but they can't. You have forgotten about it – but they have not. I couldn't say, "I didn't do it." I could tell 'em I don't remember, but as to making a plea for myself, I would be helpless.

SAL. Nobody remembers everything.

PHIL. So what I'm askin' is – you are not the fucking long arm of some guy, he's got a grudge on me – you made your customary high-priced arrangement, regarding mayhem, which is no wonder you are stress-related, Sal. I mean, if you're gonna shoot me, shoot me, okay.

SAL. I don't wanna shoot you.

PHIL. Who you gonna shoot? After all, the old broad says it's imminent.

SAL. Maybe I'll shoot her.

> *(Offering his glass.)*

Salud.

PHIL. *(They clink glasses and drink.)* You missed me?

SAL. Yeh.

PHIL. You actually missed me?

SAL. *(Moving to the swivel chair.)* I was in town, you know –

> **(SAL** *moves the blanket in order to sit, uncovering the bear.)*

– I says to myself, Phil has got to be –

> *(He stares at it, backs up a step.)*

SAL. So what's this?

PHIL. Where'd you get that?

SAL. It was here.

PHIL. It was there? It was there on the chair?

SAL. It ain't yours?

PHIL. No.

SAL. So whose is it?

PHIL. Lemme see it.

> *(Crossing to pick up the bear.)*

SAL. Yeh. You look it over. This is a teddy bear with a diaper on it, that's what we got here.

PHIL. I can see that.

SAL. Somebody hadda do it. The bear didn't do it to his pathetic self.

PHIL. Of course not.

SAL. So maybe somebody, they were passing by, they dropped him.

PHIL. Maybe.

SAL. You should lock your door, this kind of person can just wander through. Who would do such a thing?

PHIL. This is California, Sal. You gotta remember that.

> *(Settling on the couch, tossing the bear under the coffee table.)*

SAL. How do you stand it? That's the real question – how do you fuckin' stand it, Phil? That is what I come here to ask you. How do you fuckin' stand it?

PHIL. I'm gonna have another drink.

SAL. You drank that whole thing?

PHIL. Yeh. I'm gonna have another one. You want another one?

> *(Starting to make another drink.)*

SAL. I told you – this is my limit. I sense an entire other world beyond this drink – an entire other world of absolute havoc into which I am not yet ready to go.

*(He sets down the drink and moves toward
the window.)*

PHIL. So you come to California, Sal. What are you – on
vacation?

SAL. The trees, Phil. The trees are horrible out here. And
the sun.

(At the window, **SAL** *puts on his sunglasses.)*

I mean, the pavement – you're drivin' your car – you
can't see a thing for the glare. It's a wonder anybody
survives a day out here.

PHIL. I go out only at night as much as possible.

SAL. No, no, no. I'm going to be candid, Phil. I have some
work here. I can trust you, right? There's a guy – no
need to name him – he likes to get in his plane, he
flies to Vegas, right, he loses a lot of money. This is his
privilege, except he goes too far and loses money he has
already lost, but he lost track.

*(Returning, he takes up his drink and settles
in the swivel chair.)*

A lot of this is due to the toot he keeps stickin' up
his nose like it's a religious fuckin' duty – this stuff is
dangerous, so that the end result is certain people feel
talk has lost all effect on this guy, he does not think he
owes what he owes, now is the time for action. So this
is where I come in, as usual – this guy is a big deal out
here, but in our world he is a douchebag and maybe
it's where you could come in. If you're interested. You
interested?

PHIL. Whata you mean?

SAL. *(Taking off his sunglasses.)* Look, I says to myself, Phil
is out there trying to live this fucking life of a muke, he
has got to be sick of it. I will give him this opportunity.

PHIL. No.

SAL. Look, Phil. I need a little help on this thing.

(Annoyed, **SAL** *prowls off toward the kitchen,
contemptuously poking around at things.)*

SAL. There are a dozen guys, I can get them with a phone call. This is not the point. That's not what I'm talking about. What I'm talking about is, save yourself. You know? What is this life you are living here? This is shit this life

> *(He's ended up in the kitchen, holding one of Phil's books.)*

PHIL. Listen to me, Sal – can you do that?

SAL. Of course.

PHIL. *(Moving to* **SAL***, very formal, polite.)* I want to thank you for this opportunity – however, as much as I am grateful, and that is as you can imagine, a truly substantial thing – but I am done with the life.

SAL. I don't understand that.

PHIL. That's all right.

SAL. How can that be? Whata you doin' here? I mean, look at this – look at this –

> *(He throws down the book, and then moves on, tossing one disgusting thing or another – a Pamper, bra, panties – from the closet.)*

And this house – there are people, they do this. They live this way – they don't know no better, God pity them – what are they, they are mukes – this is their life. What can they do? They got no choice – but you, Phil – you have been in this world of ours, and then you have walked away, as if it meant nothing. But everybody always liked you. You know that.

PHIL. *(Moves along behind* **SAL***, picking up the book, the Pamper, the bra.)* Yeh.

SAL. Who likes you here? Huh? Your bear! Your fuckin' bear! Is this your only friend?

> *(***SAL*** *knocks some scripts from off the shelf under the picture window.)*

PHIL. Whatsamatter?

SAL. I don't understand is all! You could explain it!

PHIL. Sure.

SAL. You think you could? You really think you could do that, you could explain it to me that I would understand it, this sickness you got, you want to forget your friends!

(Storming over to **PHIL,** *who is bending to pick up a Pamper.)*

PHIL. You gonna abuse me now? Go ahead!

SAL. No! This guy – a couple weeks ago, Phil – but I can't forget about it – he comes up to me, he says, "There is this thing, and now it's a mess. You gotta handle it." This is what he's sayin' to me. "What was okay is no longer okay, and you gotta handle it."

(He crosses to the kitchen table where he left his drink.)

But the problem here is, whoever he thinks he's talkin' to, I ain't him. He thinks I'm somebody else from who I really am. I wanted to rip this guy's eyes out, he don't know me – he thinks I am some other asshole. Who I don't even know. And there we are talkin' on the corner, he's talkin' to me like I don't even exist as who I really am. Fishhook Sal!

(He slouches on the arm of the couch.)

PHIL. You mean this guy is tellin' you secrets about something in which you are not even involved?

SAL. That's right. How come it upsets me so much? I'm still upset.

PHIL. Well, a person wants to be known as themselves, Sal.

SAL. I don't know. Maybe this is the night I could have two drinks.

*(***SAL*** moves to the coffee table and starts mixing his own drink. Outside, the sun is setting, the light in the room reddening.)*

Discipline? Right? It's important. But I think I have been overboard. This is what people do. They go overboard. We were young together, Phil. A person has to think about their life sooner or later, what else is there? The horses, of course. Broads. This can take up a lot of time. But then you find yourself one day, as I did with this guy who don't know who I am. I could be anybody. You remember that kid? We took him fishin'.

*(Moving in on **PHIL**, who stands by the bar, smoking, a drink in hand.)*

You remember him, I know you do.

PHIL. Sure.

SAL. He was a good-lookin' kid. That's my life, you know. That's what I'm thinkin'. We have done those things and we were together, you and me, when we done them, where are you now? I want you to do this thing with me that I have asked you.

*(**PHIL** moves away, behind the couch, picking up the scripts **SAL** threw on the floor.)*

You remember that kid? Who was mad at him? I can't remember that? Was it Big Tommy? Maybe. But he had made somebody mad. He thinks we're out for a good time, right? He's drunk. You're drunk. It looks like we're havin' a great time. He's a charmer, right? Charm has gotten him everything he has ever gotten in his life, so he thinks it's enough, but it ain't enough to get him out of what he has got into, he don't even know it. So we're tryin' to get on with things, right? Except he's havin' such a good time, he don't wanna leave the joint. So there's this broad. He picks her up. She thinks she's going to see the underworld, right? She's this airline stewardess. From somewhere. It's not an eastern city and it's not a Southern city. I can't remember it. She's a little tipsy. I don't know what she thinks she's getting into, but she's wrong. She thinks the guy is cute. She's right on that score. He went to take a piss, right, and when he comes back, he had her. He had found her by the jukebox. They liked the same song. They were pushing the same number. It's fate. That's his line of shit. Right?

(**PHIL** *has ended in the kitchen, leaning against the refrigerator.* **SAL** *moves in on him now.*)

Now what are we gonna do? It's a mess. So we're all sittin' there, you three are drinkin', what am I doin'? I don't know. I'm worried. Who can blame me? He's of course really drunk now, and the only thing he can think of is he gotta get into her pants, right, and soon – because she's flying off to wherever in the morning. We gotta DO something. Get them outa there, right? Her name was Bobbi, right? And we are working some kind of maneuver, and – No, no. His name was Bobby. Her name was – I don't know what. Right? Am I right? So whata we tell 'em? We gotta get him outa there.

PHIL. We tell 'em we wanna go fishin'.

(**PHIL** *sits at the table.*)

SAL. He leans across to me, and I swear to God, I'll never forget this, I can see it like it was yesterday, he's so totally fucked up he's like walleyed, that's how drunk he is – and I'm thinkin' this is pathetic, this guy is going to die in such a state as this, and he's whisperin' to me how he has got to get in this broad's pants immediately and then we can go fishing, but if he is not on her bones within the hour, he is going to die of blue balls. Did you know this?

PHIL. No.

SAL. He did. He said that. He hadda fuck Bobbi the stewardess, he says. Their song was, and he named it. It was popular at the time, but it is now long forgotten. I don't remember it. But it was a group.

PHIL. He was Bobby.

SAL. Is that right?

PHIL. She was Jeananne. She was from a little town – near Cleveland.

SAL. You know what I'm sayin', Phil? A person's life is made up of such events. What did we do to them? I know we burned the car afterwards, but what did we do? I can't get it quite right so it's like this fuckin' gap, you know? It's this – gap. Somebody said somethin', we did this, we did that – I know we got them outa there. That's what I was hopin' you could help me with. Can you?

PHIL. Somethin's wrong with you, Sal.

SAL. It's just nostalgia, Phil. That's all. I just miss everybody. Like you. I want you to do this thing with me tomorrow – I feel like you're missing from what I do.

PHIL. I tole you I ain't goin' with you.

SAL. You'd rather live this shit of a life.

PHIL. If that's what you're sayin'. I just don't wanna do it anymore. Is that so hard to understand?

SAL. It's fuckin' impossible.

PHIL. I'm sorry.

>   (SAL *sits with* PHIL *at the table as the sunset is*
>   *quite far along, the dark growing; they sit in*
>   *shafts of red coming in the kitchen window.*)

SAL. So will you at least help me out with this other thing I'm tryin' to remember?

PHIL. What other thing?

SAL. Did Bobby get to fuck Jeananne before we hit them?

PHIL. Yeh.

SAL. He did.

PHIL. Except we didn't hit him. We broke his legs.

SAL. But he got to screw her.

PHIL. Yeh. Inna back seat.

SAL. But we didn't hit him?

PHIL. I never killed nobody, Sal.

SAL. You didn't? I thought you put the gun behind his ear and pulled the trigger.

PHIL. No.

SAL. I thought you did that. And we split his belly open and put him in the river.

PHIL. Could I have walked away if I had done that, Sal?

(Reaching to the kitchen light switch.)

SAL. You didn't?

PHIL. No.

*(**PHIL** throws the switch and the lights come on.)*

SAL. It musta been me, then. You quit before we got to that, huh?

PHIL. Yeh.

SAL. How could you quit without doin' that?

PHIL. I think there is somethin' wrong with you, Sal.

SAL. Yeh? Maybe. Who was so mad at him we hadda get him? You remember that?

PHIL. No.

SAL. You don't. I don't either. It was somebody, though, right.

PHIL. Of course it was somebody. Whata you think, it was nobody?

SAL. But you don't remember, I don't remember.

PHIL. Whata you think, we did it on a whim?

SAL. That's what I wanna know. Everything that happens to a person has a place somehow in their lives.

PHIL. Every fuckin' little thing?

SAL. That's why things are the way they are.

PHIL. Is that what you're sayin'? That has no basis whatsoever! I don't believe that for a minute. I mean, you can say that if you wanna, a person can say anything, but –

SAL. You think I'm fuckin' around? I'm talkin' about our lives here. That's what I believe! What do you believe – THAT EVERYTHING CAN BE FORGOTTEN?!

PHIL. I come out here to get away. If I wanted to be a crook, I coulda been one forever, but I didn't – I come out here.

SAL. But that's so fucked up, Phil. It's offensive. You're makin' me sick.

(Heading for a refill at the coffee table.)

SAL. You're gonna have me shittin' blood.

PHIL. I wanted to change my life. Where's the problem?

SAL. There ain't no problem.

(He storms back, pulling a pistol and waving it in the air.)

Am I actin' like there's a problem? Because if there was a problem, we'd be tip-toeing around your brains all over the linoleum, wouldn't we.

PHIL. *(Rising, he backs a step away.)* Sal, I had permission. I had a table. I sat down with important people, they gave their fuckin' blessing.

SAL. You had a table?

PHIL. After eight years in the slam, I had kept my tongue –

(Hurling his beer can, he storms away.)

I SPOKE OF NOTHIN' TO NOBODY! Not that I ever knew nothin' anyway –

SAL. I didn't know you had a table.

PHIL. Well, I did. This was with Arthur – no need to mention his last name and this was with Mr. Strolly and Big Tommy. "You are disenchanted," says Arthur. "I don't know," I tole him. "I think so," says Arthur. "Did you get it up the ass in the slam, you were doin' your time?" says Big Tommy. "Is that what happened to your courage, Phil? Tell us the truth," he says. You know how Big Tommy is, right. He's gotta insult everybody. So this could be a tricky moment, but I don't want trouble, and I don't want to look weak so I gotta say something insane like, "Shut up, you fat fuck, before I rip your eyes out." He smiles, of course. He's such a serious asshole. I'm thinkin', "Now what? Now what?" So we're starin' at each other.

SAL. He's dead you know.

PHIL. Who?

SAL. Big Tommy.

PHIL. He's dead?

SAL. Yeh. He disappeared.

(Taking off his jacket, he hangs it on the back of a kitchen chair.)

PHIL. He disappeared? What happened?

SAL. What? Are you worried about him?

PHIL. No, I ain't worried about him. He was just there, you know. Big Tommy. Now he's dead.

SAL. Most guys get it, Phil, they deserve it.

PHIL. Everybody deserves it. I hope you don't think you don't deserve it.

SAL. Of course I deserve it.

PHIL. Because you do, and the more you're doin' it, the more you deserve it.

(Picking up the gun, looking at it.)

I mean, in this thing of ours, what was it but a world where there was always somebody yellin' – "Hit him, kill him, whack him, hit him." Has it never occurred to you?

SAL. What?

PHIL. To get out.

SAL. And do what?

PHIL. I don't know.

SAL. What would I do?

PHIL. I don't know.

(He puts the gun back on the table and moves to wash his hands at the sink.)

That's the second part. The first part is the first part, and then you're out, you gotta worry about doin' what?

SAL. Be a muke? No thank you. I'll go to my grave smilin' before I try that. GROW UP, HUH? GROW THE FUCK UP!

PHIL. Anyway, there was other things involved. It wasn't just the fuckin' mayhem. It wasn't just the fact of the unrelenting havoc, but other things, also.

SAL. Like what?

PHIL. I had things, they were in me, these – I don't know, I don't wanna call them feelings, but they were on my mind more than I cared to admit or anyone might have known –

> *(Moving up by the window he picks up a film script, throws the light switch on by the front door.)*

I had gone to movies as a kid with a vengeance, Sal, I mean, this is why my pool game, for example, is not what a person would expect of me, because everybody was at the hall, I was at the movies. So I had this idea for a long time.

SAL. Everybody goes to the movies, Phil. I love the movies.

PHIL. That's not what I'm sayin'.

SAL. It is what you're sayin'!

PHIL. I mean, it wasn't just the goddamn movies!

SAL. I knew it. There hadda be somethin' else!

PHIL. I hated the slam, Sal.

SAL. You're supposed to hate it, you dumb fuck. That's why they make it so miserable.

PHIL. I KNOW THAT!

SAL. So whata you talkin' about then?

PHIL. I DON'T KNOW!

> *(Fleeing SAL, needing some space.)*

I wasn't inside two days, right – two days, Sal! – and there's this guy he's got a beef with me from the street, he sends his dog after me, the dog is this weight-lifter asshole who, the minute I see him take his first step toward me – this is in the chow line, right – I put my fork in his eye. Fortunately he has in his fist a shiv as I knew he would, so, though I am proven right in it was self-defense and to that extent I am exonerated, I am nevertheless put in solitary. He don't die, this fuck. So I am in solitary. I spend the whole time planning my vengeance on this asshole who provoked the whole thing to begin with, because I know he's devoting his days to imagining mayhem which he can inflict it on me, I gotta be ready. It's him or me. So I get out and do you know what?

SAL. What?

PHIL. He's dead.

SAL. The dog? The weight-lifter dog?

PHIL. No. The other guy. The instigator; and do you know what? He has killed himself.

SAL. He killed himself?

PHIL. Yeh.

SAL. Whata you mean?

PHIL. *(As* **SAL** *joins him at the table.)* The guy hung himself. He killed himself. He did it with sheets in his cell. The guy with him – the guy normally in the cell with him, he was in the infirmary, this night, so the guy took his opportunity to lynch himself. And do you know what? I felt awful.

SAL. Of course you did. That's a terrible thing.

PHIL. But, Sal, I had just spent sixty days thinking up harm to do to this guy. I shoulda wanted him dead.

SAL. That's beside the point.

PHIL. It ain't logical. Or maybe it was the dog – Maybe it was the dog that caused it.

SAL. The guy's dog?

PHIL. No, no. Tony's.

SAL. Tony?

PHIL. Yeh. That's who I'm talkin' about. Tony's dog

SAL. No, no, I mean, the weight-lifter dog – the guy's dog, the guy he hung himself, this weight-lifter dog of his you put a fork in his eye. That dog.

PHIL. No, no, I'm not talkin' about that dog.

SAL. Oh.

PHIL. I'm talkin' about a different dog, a real dog.

SAL. Oh.

PHIL. This was later. This was later after I got out of the can and somethin' happened. There was this real dog. He was Tony's dog.

SAL. Tony had a dog?

PHIL. Yeh.

SAL. I don't remember he had a dog.

PHIL. Of course he did.

SAL. When?

PHIL. Whata you mean, "When?" This dog. He was there, I got outa the can. How could you forget such a dog? Tony Bernini.

SAL. I remember Tony. I don't remember the dog.

PHIL. You hated that dog.

SAL. I don't remember him.

PHIL. Little dog.

SAL. I don't remember him.

PHIL. Bulldog. Face all scrunched up.

SAL. Oh, yeh.

PHIL. That's right.

SAL. That dog. What about him?

PHIL. I killed him.

SAL. You killed that dog? I didn't know that.

PHIL. Well, I did.

SAL. Does Tony know that?

PHIL. I don't know. But I think he does.

SAL. How come you did that? I mean, what's wrong with you, you gotta kill a poor fuckin' little dog like that?

PHIL. That's what I'm tryin' to get at, Sal, I mean, what'd I do that for? That dog was an evil fuck, of this there's no doubt, and he had it in for me, but still. I mean, he was just a nasty fuckin' little dog, but nevertheless – I mean, every time I would go in there, he would growl at me, and he would bite my shoes and my trouser cuffs. I hated him. I admit it. I'm fresh out of the slam, right? The last thing I need is this goddamn dog attacking my shoes and biting my trousers. I have been pent up for eight and a half years, then I'm out, who knows what I'm gonna do with myself, there's this goddamn dog – I mean, let's face it, let's not kid ourselves, he was a vicious little prick of a dog. So I fell asleep on Tony's couch, I'm sleepin', right? This evil fucking dog comes up to me – I got my hand like this, you know, I'm sleepin', I'm defenseless, right, he pisses on my hand. I picked him up by his collar. Like he was a guy, I held him out, I whacked him right square between the eyes. Next thing I know, he's dead. He gets this look – it's very briefly in his eyes – this look like he has been asked a question the likes of which he has never heard of it before and he ain't got a chance in hell of gettin' it right. So he looks this way, right, and next he looks for just a second at me like he loves me, and then there's this half-second in which it appears he has just remembered a very important errand he forgot to do. So these are the looks he gives. Next thing is, this blood comin' out his eyes. I'm standin' there, I have just killed this little dog with one blow, now he's like this stuffed animal, only blood is comin' out his eyes. I thought, to myself, I don't wanna do this anymore.

SAL. I always wondered what happened to that dog.

PHIL. I killed him.

SAL. Lemme ask you somethin'?

PHIL. Okay.

SAL. You know in that TV show you were on, that detective thing, where they go all over the world as if there ain't enough crooks in one place –

PHIL. Yeh?

SAL. When you were on it, that guy you were with –

PHIL. What guy?

SAL. The P.I. – the main guy –

PHIL. – Jackie! Big Jackie Garraty!

SAL. Is he a nice guy?

PHIL. Oh, yeh.

SAL. A regular guy?

PHIL. Yeh, yeh.

SAL. Can't punch for shit though, can he.

PHIL. Whata you mean?

SAL. That fight you guys had, that was shit!

PHIL. You didn't like that?

SAL. I mean, you fell good. I ain't talkin' about how you fell because it was very real how you fell – but, if you're gonna do it with this guy, at least teach him to throw a punch, because otherwise you look like some ole lady could knock you over.

PHIL. Yeh, well there's a lot goes into these things you don't know about, Sal.

SAL. I'm just sayin', I'm your average guy, I'm readin' the paper, havin' a beer at the local joint, and I look up and God as my witness, Phil, it's you in this humiliating piece of shit.

PHIL. What about that other part where I was in the parking lot and I tole Garraty he never shoulda done what he did to my brother?

SAL. This was on that show?

PHIL. Yeh! It was in the beginning – it was the set-up for the whole show.

SAL. I didn't see the beginning. I tuned in late!

PHIL. Ohhhh, you shoulda seen that! I had a close-up! Some people found it very moving. The whole episode was Garraty's got a case of the ass about my boss, see, so he's trying to provoke him by tormenting my kid brother. So he has harassed my brother until the kid is in such a frenzy he takes a punch at Garraty, then Garraty locks him up and says the kid is gone FOR FUCKING EVER, which makes me totally insane so I am –

SAL. WHAT A LOAD OF BULLSHIT, he takes advantage of some dumb kid.

PHIL. I know. That's what I'm gonna tell him! I'm behind this parked car and jump out – I wish you'd seen I got a close-up.

SAL. All I seen is this sissy swingin' at you, an' you go flyin' like he hit you with a crowbar.

PHIL. It wasn't that bad for Chrissakes!

SAL. It was horrifying! It was disgusting! The people in the bar were worried about me!

> *(Grabbing Phil's jacket from the couch, he starts to try to put it on* **PHIL.**)

They thought I was gonna throw up, or I was havin' some kind of attack. They're all runnin' up to me – "What's wrong, Sal? Are you sick, Sal?"

PHIL. *(Overlapping* **SAL** *and pulling free.)* Hey, hey, hey – the next time you look up from your pretzels and it's me up there, you wipe the foam off your nose, YOU SAVE YOURSELF, OKAY! So you don't have to endure this kind of painful experience!

SAL. WHAT AM I SUPPOSED TO DO ABOUT SUCH BULLSHIT?

PHIL. WATCH SOMETHING ELSE!

SAL. So. What the fuck. You wanna go out with me?

> *(Leaving* **PHIL**, *who stands with the coat half on,* **SAL** *heads for the kitchen to grab his own jacket from off the kitchen chair.)*

PHIL. What? No.

SAL. I gotta see somebody.

PHIL. You ain't workin' tonight. I hope you ain't workin' tonight.

SAL. *(Putting on his coat, he heads for the front door.)* We are neither one of us supposed to be on this earth at this moment of time and space, Phil. Come with me now. You don't have to worry, I don't work fucked-up.

> *(Coming down to* **PHIL**, **SAL** *grabs the bourbon bottle from the coffee table and takes a quick drink.)*

But in between – I like the blur – I like the buzz, I like the sense I am in full flight. I get from place to place, I don't know how.

(He grabs the teddy bear from the floor and stuffs it into **PHIL**'s *arms.)*

SAL. And you can take the bear. Someday somethin' will happen, and you will say, "Nobody here knows me."

(His arm around **PHIL**, *they start for the door.)*

We'll go see some mud wrestling. I love watchin' the broads playin' grab-ass in the mud, don't you. Anybody dares to mock you for on account of you got a furry animal with you we will give 'em three in the head and one in the nuts. C'mon.

*(***SAL*** opens the door, but* **PHIL** *pulls away, backs downstage.)*

PHIL. I can't.

SAL. You mean you won't – you refuse.

PHIL. Whatever.

(Angrily, **SAL** *sets the bourbon bottle down on the shelves by the door.)*

SAL. Okay, sure. But lemme ask you one thing. I mean, I was you and I was out here and I couldn't get a better part than I gotta get dumped on my ass by this fairy who don't even hit me, I would shoot myself square in the fucking face! You know what I'm sayin' to you.

PHIL. Sure.

SAL. You gotta get bigger parts, Phil. You got assholes working for you, FIRE THEM! Make people know your worth! Bigger, better parts! BIGGER BETTER PARTS! An' the bad guys should win sometimes. You know that! I mean, SOMETIMES! Enough already with we-can't-drive – we-can't-shoot – we-can't-fight. You agree with me, don't you?

PHIL. Of course.

*(***SAL*** walks to the open door and stops.)*

SAL. Is there a Catholic Church around here that you know of?

PHIL. Sure. Why?

SAL. I wanna go to one. I wanna light a candle for you, Phil. I'm gonna pray for you, Phil.

PHIL. What for?

SAL. So you can help yourself is what for. That's what for.

PHIL. Maybe you should pray for yourself, Sal.

SAL. No. No. I am beyond prayer. I'm gonna do it for you. I'm gonna pray for you. And then I'm gonna light a candle for you and then I'm gonna pray for you. So where would this Catholic Church that you know of be if it's around here?

PHIL. They won't be open.

SAL. Why?

PHIL. It's too late.

SAL. What time is it?

PHIL. *(Looking at his watch.)* They won't be open.

SAL. No.

> *(Looking at his watch.)*

They won't be open. Well, some other time, then.

> *(They both stand looking at their watches.)*
> *(Blackout.)*

Scene Three

> (**PHIL** *is lying on the couch in dim light.*
> *The bear is upstage by the window on the*
> *bookshelves.* **SUSIE** *opens the door and peeks*
> *in. She is dressed as she was when she left.*
> **PHIL** *wears trousers, t-shirt. No shoes.*)

SUSIE. Hi.

> (*As she puts her keys and pocketbook on table*
> *by door.*)

Phil, honey? You sleepin', honey?

> (*Removing her jacket, she hangs it in closet.*)

PHIL. No.

SUSIE. Whata you been doin'?

PHIL. Ohhh, nothin'. You know. Thinkin'. You know.

SUSIE. Sure.

> (*Looking over the apartment, feeling*
> *something amiss or out of place.*)

Did something happen while I was gone?

> (*Continuing to feel odd, looking around.*)

What happened while I was gone?

PHIL. Nothin'. Just...you know. What'd you do?

SUSIE. (*Crosses to the couch next to* **PHIL,** *with her purse.*)
We just went out for dinner. To this – it was a Mexican
place. I'd never been there before. Janice knew about it.

> (*Feeling pressure in her stomach, she flinches.*)

PHIL. Any good?

SUSIE. Great.

> (*Heading for the kitchen, she takes a*
> *thermometer from her purse and puts it in*
> *her mouth.*)

You wanna watch some TV in a little?

PHIL. No. Maybe.

(**PHIL** *grabs the elocution book from a pile of scripts near the door as* **SUSIE** *turns on a light in the kitchen.*)

I was tryin' to work on my voice, you know. My elocution, you know. There's no doubt about it, I need work in that area. "Which whelp whined when he heard the whale wheeze."

(*Meeting eyes with* **SUSIE**.)

I'm tryin'.

SUSIE. It's good.

(*In the kitchen cleaning up, the thermometer in her mouth.*)

PHIL. "A coward weeps and wails with woe when his wiles are thwarted."

(*Moving to the couch, as in the kitchen,* **SUSIE** *removes the thermometer and looks at it.*)

The pelican's pouch is primarily appropriate for keeping him –

SUSIE. Phil! PHIL!

PHIL. What?

SUSIE. Phil, Phil! I'm ovulating.

(*She runs to him on the couch.*)

My temperature is perfect. I've been feeling strange all day, but –

PHIL. What's it say?

SUSIE. C'mon. It's perfect. It's perfect.

PHIL. You says it was over.

SUSIE. I almost didn't take my temperature I mean, I thought the way I felt and all, that it was over, but that wasn't what it meant at all.

PHIL. (*Takes the thermometer.*) What did it mean?

SUSIE. And then it was like something almost hit me; it almost hurt.

(*As she stands, drawing him to stand with her.*)

PHIL. What did that mean?

SUSIE. Oh, boy, oh, boy, I mean, we almost missed this.

> *(Hand in hand, they head to the bedroom, but as she enters, he gently pulls free. She calls from off.)*

(Offstage.) Do you want some grass? Phil? Phil!

PHIL. *(Retreating to the liquor cabinet.)* I gotta get something.

SUSIE. *(Offstage.)* Hurry up.

> *(Entering, partially undressed.)*

Phil.

PHIL. What?

> *(As he pours a drink, she sees him.)*

SUSIE. What are you doing?

PHIL. I want a drink. You want a drink?

SUSIE. *(Moving to him.)* Phil, honey, what's going on?

PHIL. I want a drink is what's going on. Is that so hard to understand?

SUSIE. But why do you have to have it now?

PHIL. Because I want it now, so it's only logical that I have it now.

SUSIE. I mean, you don't think there's something a little wrong here. We go in there to, you know, make love and next thing we know we're out here, you have to have a drink.

PHIL. So?

SUSIE. Ohhh, we're going to miss it; we're going to miss it.

> *(Flirting with him, playfully, she gets him moving again.)*

PHIL. No, we won't.

SUSIE. Please. We only have an hour.

PHIL. I wanna have my drink, okay?

> *(Pulling free.)*

SUSIE. Why? Because it might actually work, is that the problem, and I might actually get pregnant. Is that why you're stalling?

PHIL. I'm not stalling.

SUSIE. Then what are you doing?

PHIL. I DON'T KNOW.

> *(**SUSIE** storms to the kitchen, where she flops down at the table.)*

Susie, honey, just listen to me. Just listen to me. PLEASE just listen to me.

SUSIE. I am listening to you.

PHIL. Just, please, please, okay, please.

SUSIE. I am listening to you. But what are you, I mean, SAYING, except what? WHAT? Okay? I mean, I'm trying to listen to you but you're just asking me to listen to you.

> *(She gets Valium from her purse that is hanging over the chair.)*

PHIL. You're right. You're absolutely right.

> *(Moving to her.)*

I'm beggin' you, don't cry. What are you doing?

SUSIE. I'm taking a Valium, okay? If you don't mind, unless that's something you're just, you know, OPPOSED TO, for your, you know, UNKNOWN REASONS, who knows what they are. I'm upset. You're upsetting me. And I'll cry if I feel like it. I feel awful.

> *(She takes a pill with a drink.)*

PHIL. It just makes it hard for me to think, you know. Your cryin'.

SUSIE. Don't pay any attention to it.

PHIL. How can I not pay any attention to the fact that you are cryin' right in front of me.

SUSIE. You don't pay any attention to anything else about me.

(Rushing to the couch, she flops down.)

PHIL. Ohhh, Susie, c'mon.

SUSIE. You don't. You just ignore everything important to me. Why are you doing this? You're ruining everything.

PHIL. I'm not ruinin' nothin'.

(Joins her, trying to comfort her, but she pulls back.)

SUSIE. Well, what I have to say to you okay, is HERE'S what I have to say – IF this is some sort of fait accompli, this goddamn decision and it's, you know, MADE, well, I have a right to know it – because if you have categorically decided you don't want to have a baby, it is your moral obligation that you tell me okay, because then I have some decisions to make too.

PHIL. I mean, everything's gonna be okay, Susie.

SUSIE. I want you to be totally, completely honest with me, Phil? Can you do that?

PHIL. Everything's gonna be fine, Susie.

SUSIE. How can you say that?

PHIL. Because it is! Like what kind of decisions would you have to make?

SUSIE. I mean, you promised, Phil. When we got married, you promised we could have a baby.

PHIL. I know that.

SUSIE. Well, you have to keep your word.

PHIL. I know that.

SUSIE. *(Moving closer to him on the couch.)* Well you have to then. All right? All right, honey?

PHIL. Okay.

SUSIE. C'mon, honey. C'mon.

(She tugs up his shirt, kisses his stomach.)

We'll have fun. You'll love a little baby.

(She kisses him as he undoes his belt; together, they tug his trousers down.)

PHIL. I know, I know. But the world's such a mess.

SUSIE. The what?

(Standing on the couch, pulling off her pantyhose.)

PHIL. World.

SUSIE. The world?

PHIL. Yeh.

SUSIE. You're worried about the world?

PHIL. You know. The Mideast. Anything could happen. People are angry all over the world. Everybody's got the bomb.

SUSIE. Ohhh, that's so sweet, Phil –

(She climbs onto his lap, kisses him, sitting, straddling him.)

That's so cute; you're worried about the world. You don't want our little baby getting born into a terrible world. You don't even know what a sweetheart you really are sometimes, do you. But you are. You wanna fuck, though, don't you. You wanna do that. Huh? Sure you do.

(On him, she leans into a long kiss.)

PHIL. Goddamnit. Goddamnit, goddamnit, goddamnit.

(He leaps up, pulling his pants up.)

SUSIE. How can you do this to me? I'll kill myself, Phil. I will. I'll kill myself. I swear I will. You promised. Didn't you promise we could have a baby. Didn't you make me that promise?

PHIL. You're right. I'm not sayin' you're not RIGHT. You're right, Susie.

SUSIE. Were you lying to me?

PHIL. No.

SUSIE. I mean, was it a trick?

PHIL. I don't think so. I don't.

SUSIE. One of your jokes you and Eddie and the rest of your asshole buddies think you have to play on Susie? "Pathetic little Susie"!

>*(**SUSIE** hits **PHIL** with a sofa pillow.)*

PHIL. No.

SUSIE. That fucking Eddie! Just to make a fool out of me!

PHIL. He's important to my career, Susie.

>*(Grabbing his jacket, he heads for the door.)*

And he likes you. He –

SUSIE. Ohhh, I'm so upset! I feel like I'm going to be sick. THEN WHAT IS IT?

PHIL. I DON'T KNOW.

>*(Hurling the door open, he goes.)*

SUSIE. Bullshit.

>*(She slams the door behind him and starts for the bedroom, getting only a couple of steps before the door swings open and he's back in.)*

PHIL. I want my turn. I just keep thinkin' I want my turn. I never had my turn, you know where it's just you and me. You look at me and talk to me.

SUSIE. I want that.

>*(She moves to him; fits into his arms.)*

PHIL. Susie, listen to me, I mean, if we don't have a kid then what?

SUSIE. You are really hurting my feelings! How can I forgive you for this?!

>*(She pulls free of him, grabbing the teddy bear from the windowsill and heading for the kitchen.)*

I don't know how I'm ever going to be able to forgive you for this, Phil.

>*(At the kitchen table she sits and takes Valium, as he approaches.)*

PHIL. I'm not sayin', you know, "NO." I'm not sayin' that: categorically, you know, "NO," or "NEVER," I'm not sayin' that.

SUSIE. You're not?

PHIL. No. No, no.

SUSIE. What are you saying?

PHIL. What am I saying? I'm saying – I mean, what I'm saying is – ONE THING is – one thing I'm saying is I'm already a shit father to three kids, you know.

(Moving away.)

That's one thing. I'm maybe the worst goddamn father on the face of the earth, that's one thing. We both know that. I mean, there's no arguin' that. I mean, I don't even know where they are? They could be anywhere. I could meet 'em on the street tomorrow, you know, they're walkin' along the strip, I don't even know them. That's one thing.

SUSIE. But you and your wife didn't love each other, Phil. We love each other. I mean, you love me, don't you?

PHIL. That's what I'm saying.

(As he stops, she moves into his arms.)

But anybody can get divorced, Susie. It can happen.

SUSIE. I wouldn't. I'd never divorce you.

PHIL. But, I mean, what about those decisions you said you hadda make? Remember? What were they?

SUSIE. But that would only be if we didn't have a baby.

PHIL. Oh.

SUSIE. I mean, the baby would be like – he would be like this expression of our love.

PHIL. Sometimes, you know, I feel like my kids – I mean, my other kids, they're like doin' nothin' with their lives, but they hate me. That's what they do. It's their career – they hate me.

*(Drifting, **SUSIE** sags with the bear onto the swivel chair.)*

PHIL. Day in and day out, they're lookin' outa this sick fuckin' hate, you know, like these dogs they been kicked every day and I'm the one who every day I kicked 'em.

SUSIE. What happened to the bear?

PHIL. Did something happen to him?

SUSIE. He's all wet.

    (She sniffs the bear.)

Did you spill whiskey on him? He smells of whiskey.

PHIL. What happened to him? Lemme see him.

    (He takes the bear.)

He's wet.

SUSIE. *(Taking the bear back.)* Somebody spilled whiskey on him.

PHIL. I must have.

    (**PHIL** *moves to liquor cabinet, pours himself a drink.)*

SUSIE. How much have you been drinking?

    (Pulling the wet diaper off the bear, she tosses it onto the floor.)

PHIL. Why?

SUSIE. I want to know.

PHIL. I wasn't counting.

    (From atop the refrigerator she snatches a fresh Pamper and returns to the swivel chair to change the bear.)

SUSIE. Are you drunk?

PHIL. No. No, no. I mean, I oughta be. I mean, I COULD be, I sure as hell would be justified if I was in such a world of betrayal as this one.

SUSIE. What?

PHIL. *(Standing by the bar, drinking.)* Where old scores cannot be settled except by betrayal and blood! And there is not a friend you can have who if they have the leverage on him, they can make him forget he is your friend – or not forget, they don't care, but he will take you to where they are waiting, and he will give you to them, because when they are looking to do away with you, they do it.

SUSIE. What're you talkin' about now?

PHIL. The world. The world is a terrible place – it's terrible.

SUSIE. I know it is.

PHIL. No, no, it's worse than that. Worse than you can imagine.

SUSIE. I know that.

PHIL. You can't know it's worse than you can imagine. How you gonna know that?

SUSIE. I know what it is. I'm not stupid.

PHIL. I'm not sayin' you're stupid. It's stupid to know it. I'm stupid. I'm the stupid one.

(He sags to sit on the edge of the coffee table.)

I been around enough to know what a lowlife excuse for a world this world of swindle is because what's done is done when you have made your last mistake is where some poor kid can just get into the wrong car.

SUSIE. Whatsamatter?

PHIL. I love you, Susie. I love you.

(Leaving the bear seated on the swivel chair, SUSIE *moves between the chair and the coffee table; she kneels on the floor before* PHIL *as he talks.)*

Sometimes I think about you all day long, and you're in thoughts I don't even want you in them, and I don't know how I ever had the blind luck that got me in with you – I don't – I swear I don't, but –

SUSIE. Ohhh, honey, you can be such a sweetie sometimes.

PHIL. Don't be mad at me.

SUSIE. Can't you be a sweetie all the time, and not just some of the time?

PHIL. Let's just forget about everything, okay. Just forget about it.

SUSIE. I wanna.

> *(As she lies back on floor.)*

PHIL. I wanna.

> *(Settling down on top of her. They kiss.)*

SUSIE. I'm just glad we straightened everything out.

PHIL. Yeh.

> *(They kiss.)*

Susie...?

SUSIE. Mmmmmm?

PHIL. Put in your diaphragm, okay?

SUSIE. Sure.

> *(After a little kiss, she looks at him.)*

I did already.

PHIL. Oh.

> *(They kiss. He stops.)*

Susie, when?

SUSIE. What?

PHIL. You put it in already?

SUSIE. Yes.

PHIL. Oh.

> *(They kiss, and then he pulls back.)*

When did you do that?

SUSIE. I mean, I will.

PHIL. Okay.

> *(She runs into bathroom.)*

I wanna see you do it.

SUSIE. *(Offstage.)* What?

PHIL. I wanna see you do it.

SUSIE. *(Comes out of bathroom carrying her diaphragm and spermicide.)* Do what?

PHIL. Susie, you know do what. What are we talkin' about? I wanna see it.

SUSIE. *(As she fills the diaphragm with spermicide.)* Phil, if I was tryin' to trick you, I could just put little holes in it.

PHIL. Susie?

SUSIE. What?

PHIL. *(Taking the diaphragm, examining it.)* Did you do that?

SUSIE. What's wrong with you? I wouldn't trick you. Do you think I'd do that? That's really insulting if you do. Why are you just ruining things over and over?

PHIL. I don't know.

SUSIE. I mean, you promised me. What am I supposed to do? I'm almost thirty-three years old.

PHIL. Whata you talkin' about? You think that's old? That's not –

SUSIE. But if I'm married to you and you won't ever, I might as well be sixty. I might as well be a hundred and –

PHIL. I never said "won't ever." You cannot say I ever said that. I never –

SUSIE. You think I'm just so small-minded and stupid, I can't stand it!

> *(**SUSIE** moves into kitchen, takes another Valium.)*

PHIL. You wouldn't wanna do it to me! I'm not sayin', you Susie personally would wanna trick me. But somethin' would. I don't know what makes people do things, but somethin' does and they do them. Somethin' jumps in 'em outa the air – or the moon, or their fuckin' chromosomes – their X's, their Y's, their bullshit.

> *(Reeling onto the couch, he sees the bear in its diaper on the swivel chair.)*

I mean look at this fuckin' bear! Where does he think he's goin'? If you don't know what I'm talking about, why is this goddamned bear dressed up like this? THE BABY WOULD MAKE YOU DO IT!

SUSIE. What baby?

PHIL. Whata you gonna pass out on me here? You gonna sleepwalk on me?

SUSIE. WHAT BABY?

PHIL. The baby we are forever talking about. That baby. The baby he would be the embodiment of our love. That baby.

SUSIE. He ain't real.

> *(Grabbing the bear, she flops onto the swivel chair.)*

PHIL. That's exactly what I'm talkin' about!

> *(The night sky in the window is strange, all moon and icy light.)*

He would be this goddamn invisible, unrelenting motherfucker of a baby, this goddamn idea baby in your head who would be tough, and he would be stubborn, and it wouldn't matter was he or wasn't he real, because he could like reach unseen into your brain and get a hold'a you in the perfect place so he had you where he wanted you and you would be putty in his hands.

> *(Gesturing, **PHIL** knocks a glass of ice and bourbon from the edge of the coffee table to the floor.)*

SUSIE. Oh dammit! Now what did you do, Phil?

> *(She kneels to wipe the mess with the diaper nearby.)*

PHIL. Do? What did I do? NOTHIN'! I mean, people don't DO everything, you know. It looks like they do! But they don't. There are some things, THEY JUST HAPPEN.

> *(Deliberately, he knocks another drink over.)*

And people are – They're IN THEM. They're not DOING THEM. They're in them. And they happen, these things that look like these people are doin' them – these things are in fact happening TO these people...

> *(As **SUSIE** wipes the mess, he talks to her.)*

...along with the other people who are obviously being done to by the people it looks like are doing these things. I mean, who has not heard somebody say, "I didn't know I was going to do that." Everybody has said it. And do you know what? THEY didn't know it either – BECAUSE – do you know why? – THEY DIDN'T DO IT! There's like these other guys and I don't know who they are, nobody knows who they are – but THEY DO IT! Who are these fuckin' guys, they do it, they hide, I take the heat?!

(**PHIL** *grabs the bear and won't let* **SUSIE** *get it back.*)

There's this broad in West L.A., right, she believes her eight-month-old baby is the devil, right, so she puts him in the oven. She cooks her baby because she thinks he is the devil. Whata you think'a that? You think you couldn't, don't you, but that's what you don't know, because you're an asshole, and you could, ANYBODY! They could!

(*She can't get the bear and flees into the bedroom.*)

I'd love to hear your goddamn theory! Okay, Doctor Susie! I THOUGHT YOU KNEW ABOUT THIS! Susie Einstein! Huh? Susie Big Brain, I-been-to-one-year-a-college. I mean, everybody says, "Oh, sure. Right. My unconscious. I did it unconsciously."

(*To the bear.*) What are they talking about? This big fucking wind it is about to push them off the earth. This goddamn wind comes up out of them, and it blows their brains away. And what is going to stop them then?

(*He shakes the bear as if it is in the wind.*)

What are they going to do against this wind which it is absolutely one hundred percent something they-don't-know-what – but it blows their hearts right out of them and there they are then left like that, and it's cold. What are they going to do then? Huh? And it ain't just now I'm talkin' about.

(Seated, explaining to the bear.)

PHIL. But HISTORY. Now! SURE! Of course, NOW! I mean, Genghis Khan would torch you in your bed as well now as later, give him an opportunity, he's got his hard-on. Or you think the Arabs or the Iranians or one'a these Third World tribal motherfuckers will not hunt you down if you do the one thing whatever-it-is which in their minds is this proof beyond all doubt that you have hurt them so they must have you where they want you which is dead and your belly slit open...

(With his finger, he mimes slitting the bear's belly open.)

...in order that when they dump you in the river, the river will keep you, because the water will not let you go if your belly is slashed...and no one will ever see you again.

SUSIE. *(Returns in pajamas and a robe.)* Yaaba...ddda...yabba...da...blah blah is all you ever say.

PHIL. I mean, you don't wanna hear about the past, okay, forget the past. I mean, FORGET IT! The past is the past, who needs it?

(He gives her the bear and she moves to the bedroom.)

SUSIE. I'm goin' to bed. It's so mean what you're saying. It's so mean.

PHIL. People! I'm talkin' about people. I mean, Anthony Augusto! I mean, Arthur Pauley Downs! I mean, Hitler! I mean, Genghis Kahn! THEY WERE THE WIND!

(Having followed her until she shut the door, he looks out the picture window at the cold night sky, a moon filling the room with icy light.)

And you wanna bring a little person to this place, they can be a part of that. What are you, nuts? Are you insane?

(He sits on the window seat.)

I mean, sometimes we would worry, Susie, you know, we was just little kids at night, little kids sittin' on the stoop at night and we was worried – what would be the next ice age. We was just little kids and we would wonder, would it be earthquakes or fire or flood? What would it be? What?

(*As* **SUSIE** *moves from the bedroom to the kitchen and picks up the phone.*)

Where you goin'? What are you doin'?

SUSIE. I wanna call Janice.

PHIL. But I'm tryin' to tell you somethin' here, Susie!

SUSIE. (*With the phone on the kitchen table she starts dialing.*) I wanna talk to her – I wanna call her up and talk to her, she's my friend!

PHIL. I don't want you callin' that goddamn Janice.

SUSIE. I mean, just because you ain't makin' any sense does not mean you are philosophical, okay? I hope you understand that!

(*They struggle for the phone; she lunges to pull free as he lets go; the phone goes flying and she bumps into the chair with books on it. Everything spills onto the floor.*)

Owwwwww, owwwww. I hurt myself. I mean, look at this crap. What is this bullshit?

(*Grabbing the books, she hurls one to the floor.*)

What's it even doing here?

PHIL. Be careful with them, will you.

SUSIE. Why? It's a joke you have these.

PHIL. (*Tries to get the books back as she moves away.*) This guy said I should read them, this director, they would reflect my life, he said –

SUSIE. You SHOULD read them, the guy is right. Who is this – they're all the same guy, this Doesty – Dusty – What a name?

PHIL. Gimme the goddamn books, Susie!

(He grabs one of the books and she dances away with the others.)

SUSIE. Oh, I got it. Here's the one the guy was talking about to reflect your life, Phil. "THE IDIOT"! The guy is right about this one. "The fucking IDIOT" would reflect your life!

PHIL. He was in prison, this guy, he was a gambler! He wrote – this is *Notes from the Underworld.*

SUSIE. "Ground," Phil. "Under Ground"!

(Realizing his error, he spins away.)

You can't even read the title, 'cause there are words in 'em got more letters than FUCK, which is your usual vocabulary, such as "shit" and –

PHIL. *(Overlapping.)* I can read 'em!

(Grabbing her, shaking her.)

Shut up! Shut up!

SUSIE. *(Overlapping.)* Give up! Give up! You ex-con deadhead! GIVE UP!

(He throws her, screaming, to the floor.)

PHIL. What'samatter with you?

SUSIE. Get out! Get out! I hope you die! I hope you die!

PHIL. Hey! Dreams can come true! YOU HEAR ME, YOU NASTY BITCH! Call Janice and tell her that! Dreams can come true!

(He goes out the front door, slamming it. Sobbing, she sits up, looking after him.)

(Music.*)

End of Act I

---

*A license to produce *Those the River Keeps* does not include a performance license for any third-party or copyrighted music. Licensees should create an original composition or use music in the public domain. For further information, please see Music Use Note on page 3.

ACT II

Scene One

(Music.* The lights rise to find **SAL**, *wearing the same dark suit and tie and his sunglasses, standing upstage near the window. The set is the mess it ended up in at the end of Act I, the chair on its side, the books and phone on the floor. Drinks, glasses, diaper, diaphragm.* **SAL** *removes his sunglasses as he takes the scene in. As the music comes to an end he strides forward to the closet by the bedroom and opens the door, as the phone rings.* **SAL** *stops, looks, as the machine picks up. He listens briefly to* **PHIL**'s *voice over the machine.)*

PHIL'S VOICE. Listen, Susie, Honey, it's Phil. Are you there, Honey? If you're there, you pick up, okay. C'mon, Hon, I'm beggin'.

*(**SAL** moves on into the closet, rooting around.)*

I'm beggin', okay, pick up, pick up if you're there. I'm comin' by in a little. It's about four-fifteen.

*(**SAL** emerges with a suit in a garment bag. He unzips the bag, taking out the suit, tossing the bag back into the closet. He studies the suit.)*

---

*A license to produce *Those the River Keeps* does not include a performance license for any third-party or copyrighted music. Licensees should create an original composition or use music in the public domain. For further information, please see Music Use Note on page 3.

PHIL'S VOICE. I'm gonna be by within the hour on accounta I gotta pick up some stuff – if you're there an' I come by we can talk.

> (**SAL** *walks to the liquor cabinet, carrying the suit. He hangs it on a hook by the other closet and starts to pour a drink.*)

I hope you're there – but if you're not, and you get this, I won't be there long. I'll just get my stuff and get out.

> (**SAL** *hears keys in the lock of the front door. Looking hastily about, he grabs the suit and slips into the closet, shutting the door as the front door opens and* **JANICE** *enters, carrying a purse, a fancy gym bag.*)

JANICE. Hello?

> (*She wears sunglasses, jeans, cowboy boots, a vest. She jingles her keys and crosses toward the bedroom door.*)

Phil? Hello?

> (*Turning, calling to the front door.*)

It's okay.

> (**SUSIE** *enters, carrying her purse and the bear, wearing a blue waitress's uniform.*)

SUSIE. I bet he calls while we're here. Every time I check there's four or five messages.

JANICE. He's such an asshole.

SUSIE. He's such an asshole. He loves me, he's sorry – that's the message – I gotta just let him see me.

> (*Approaching the machine, she sees the red light blinking.*)

See, it's just blinking and blinking.

JANICE. I hope you don't wanna hear his stupid voice and his asshole excuse, blah blah blah.

SUSIE. (*Staring at the machine.*) Blah blah blah. Let him pick up his own damn messages.

*(She marches to the refrigerator and pulls out
a bottle of wine.)*

JANICE. Listen, why don't we take a trip on the weekend?
Heather's having a party Saturday at her sister's up in
Trancus. I already got a sitter. We could stay over. You
wanna?

SUSIE. Who's gonna be there?

*(The phone rings, and they both jump as the
machine picks up.)*

PHIL'S VOICE. Susie, listen, Susie, honey, I was just hopin'
you might be there, you know.

*(As **SUSIE**, having poured two glasses of wine,
brings one to **JANICE**.)*

You might have come in, that's all. I just felt maybe.
Anyway, you gotta get these messages sooner or later.
I'm sorry, see. I'm really sorry.

JANICE. You oughta be sorry.

PHIL'S VOICE. If we could just talk? Don't you wanna talk,
Susie, honey. C'mon. I wanna talk. I wanna see you,
and talk, Susie, honey? I'm talkin' now in case you're
listenin' and –

(Listening, the girls get the giggles.)

JANICE. I mean, you oughta be relieved. It's finally over.

SUSIE. I know.

JANICE. We're sick of you! Shut up!

(She turns down the volume.)

Have you figured out what you're going to pack? Why
don't you pack with Heather and the beach in mind?
We'd have a good time. That's one thing Heather knows
how to do is have a good time.

SUSIE. *(Heading for the bedroom.)* I'm just gonna grab
some stuff.

JANICE. No, no. Pack with some kind of plan.

SUSIE. Plan? Plan for what?

*(From the closet outside the bedroom, **JANICE** gathers an armful of garments.)*

JANICE. I mean, imagine the various possibilities – picture yourself gorgeous in every occasion and pack accordingly.

SUSIE. I don't feel very gorgeous.

(Coming out of the bedroom with a suitcase and an armful of clothing.)

JANICE. Susie, honey, listen to yourself! This is what happens to a perfectly wonderful person when they have spent too much time locked up with a guy like Phil. Your self-worth starts to rot!

SUSIE. You think that's what's happening to me?

JANICE. Watching you in this marriage almost gave me a rash, Susie.

SUSIE. You were very loyal, though.

JANICE. I know. But on those nights when recently I didn't return your calls right away – I felt awful – but there were nights when I was just plain scared that I didn't have the necessary immunities, and I would feel, for godsake, what if it's contagious? What if this self-deluded way Susie has of relating to her own needs and what are other people's worst traits is some kind of communicable disease? What if it's catching?

SUSIE. Was I that bad?

(At the couch they sort what to pack.)

JANICE. Yes, you were. Not that I haven't spent years trying to exit the freeway by means of the On Ramp, myself. No, no, I mean, I know if you want to waste several years in a demented relationship you have to pick the guy with great care.

SUSIE. That's right – you have to say, "No, no, not him. Too tall. Too handsome. Too nice. Too considerate. No, no, there he is. That one. PHIL!"

JANICE. Except with this clown, it looked to me like you were determined to take the art of masochistic bullshit into some new and untested limits. I mean, can you

imagine how macabre you looked – for me to feel that I
had lost all points of personal reference?

> (**JANICE** *moves about, picking up the books,
> the diaphragm, setting them on the coffee
> table.*)

SUSIE. Yeah. It must have been so hard for you.

JANICE. *(As she stands the swivel chair upright and sits
down in it.)* It was very disorienting. I mean, when we
first met all we talked about was how much we had in
common.

SUSIE. We were like soul mates.

> *(She moves to join **JANICE** in the swivel chair
> and they sit together, pivoting side to side as
> they talk.)*

JANICE. You remember how mad you got at me that first
time I told you how I honestly felt about Phil?

SUSIE. That was so scary.

JANICE. That was almost the end for us, if you remember.

SUSIE. It was that time on the phone.

JANICE. No, no, it started on the phone, but it quickly got
too heavy, so we had to meet at that cute little bar with
the whale motif.

SUSIE. And drank twenty-seven cappuccinos apiece, because
we didn't want to drink wine, and get soused while
talking about such an important subject. Phil and I had
been married how long then?

JANICE. No, no, no!

> *(Leaping up, she moves back to the couch to
> get on with packing.)*

That was the whole point. You WEREN'T married –
you were THINKING ABOUT getting married. You
had met him and moved in with him, but – you were in
that little apartment in West Hollywood, the one with
the phony Mexican door and the sickening pea-green
shag rug.

SUSIE. *(Heading for the kitchen.)* That was the kitchen so big for so few square feet and wisteria on the front walls.

JANICE. Right. And across the street The Tart, Clarice.

SUSIE. *(Pouring another glass of wine.)* Oh, God, poor Clarice!

JANICE. With her vinyl pedal pushers and her ever-expanding thunder thighs. God, what a parade of nightmare pricks that went in and out of that place.

SUSIE. *(Joining* **JANICE** *packing on the couch.)* She was like the prototype for some form of advanced slut.

JANICE. And her only criteria in men was that they have dented cars and trashy clothes. It was probably this constant display of riffraff across your street that made Phil, by comparison, look human.

> *(This makes* **SUSIE** *laugh hard.)*

So there you are talking about marrying this guy and the whole horrific scenario is like in electric color right before my eyes. I mean, if ever there was a Gumba who, they should not have let his antecedents off Ellis Island – it was this guy. But I could not get through to you. It was like some hidden adversary was jamming my signals. Then you start screaming at me.

SUSIE. I just got so crazy.

JANICE. You're standing there screeching that you would not stand for me to talk to you and judge you like that.

SUSIE. That was how I felt.

JANICE. But I wasn't judging you I kept trying to tell you. I was judging him, I was warning you.

SUSIE. I just was so in love with him. How did you stand it?

JANICE. I don't know! And then you went into the baby madness!

> *(Grabbing up the bear.)*

And I thought, "She's berserk. This is paranormal." I wanted to ask you, do you care nothing for the aesthetic requirements of the world? I mean, the Environmental Protection Agency is going to post your name on some official penalties list you start procreating with this set of chromosomes, they have a face like a cannoli, somebody took a bite out of it – they threw it away, somebody else stepped on it, his nose is what's left.

> *(Thrusting the bear into* **SUSIE***'s arms,* **JANICE** *strides up to the shelves by the window, where she finds a bikini.)*

I mean, there we were – in the land of surfer-bodies, the land of the lean, the sun-tanned and the blonde – guys who were the product of the beach and Vitapacks and oil and nautilus, and there you were in this adolescent snit over this meatball from an unknown planet, he should not have left Mulberry Street! It was incomprehensible!

SUSIE. You know, Janice, I think maybe – *(She stops.)*

JANICE. What?

SUSIE. No, no, I was going to say something, but I think I shouldn't.

JANICE. Will you give me a break here, for godsake? I always want to know what you're thinking. It's very important to me.

SUSIE. Well, I just SORTA feel – I mean RIGHT NOW I feel, and I'm sure I'll feel differently in a couple weeks or more, or months anyway if not weeks – but right now I think maybe you are trashing Phil a little unnecessarily. Being a little –

JANICE. Are you serious?

SUSIE. It's just what I feel, and I said I didn't want to fight with you, okay. So I don't.

JANICE. I don't either – I just need to know what you're suggesting – I mean, you are not suggesting that you have taken offense because I have defamed this bozo?

SUSIE. Have I not established the fact – I hope I have established the fact – I have been trying to establish the fact that I don't want to talk about this anymore.

> *(***SUSIE** *leaps up.)*

JANICE. Why?

SUSIE. *(At the bedroom closet, she grabs a laundry bag.)* Because I don't wanna fight with anybody anymore. I'm seriously, like opposed to fighting from this day forward, okay. It gets me nowhere. It's just all this screaming, and you might as well, you know, drink Drano. You might as well put your hand in the garbage disposal and stick a fork in your eye.

> *(Flopping down in the swivel chair, she sorts the clothing.)*

JANICE. We're not fighting.

SUSIE. Oh, sure, that's easy for you to say, but I am, in my heart – see – sick of everybody being mad at me because I'm just trying to live my pathetic little life, you know, and fulfill a few of my ridiculous – I know they are – dreams – but if I have wanted something, and it's in my head, like what am I supposed to do? I can't help it how I feel.

JANICE. Just because a person tries to point out certain things you might rather avoid does not mean they are fighting with you.

SUSIE. Well, I think you are. Can I tell you something? I think you're trying to see how far you can push what is your own personal individual animosity about Phil, and this is just an opportunity for you, and you have lost track of the fact that my marriage is maybe disappearing from the planet. But I don't hate him. You hate him.

JANICE. You're the one he pushed around – unless you've forgotten that? I'm just saying good riddance.

SUSIE. Well say it nicer, okay.

JANICE. I should say good riddance nicer? Is that what you're saying?

SUSIE. See, you're attacking me. You're so goddamn judgmental, Janice. I can't stand it.

> *(As **JANICE** flees to the kitchen to refill her wine glass.)*

I feel like you just feel everything I do is stupid and everything I say and everything I think, and you feel my hair is stupid and my house and furniture. And my husband is stupid!

JANICE. Your husband is stupid. And you do have a tendency to want sort of chintzy pieces, Susie. But that's okay. That was one of the first things we had a lot of fun with together, the fact that you wanted me to educate you a little about interior decorating. I mean, it wasn't a big deal. We just did it. But you know every nice piece you have is something we picked out together.

SUSIE. But I like some of my own things – some of the things I picked out on my own. I like some of them a lot.

(Sitting down on the couch.)

JANICE. *(Joining her, trying patiently to explain.)* But you told me you wanted everything replaced if I thought it clashed or lacked pizzazz. That's what you told me.

SUSIE. Because you're so goddamn self-centered I told you.

JANICE. What?

SUSIE. I knew it was what you wanted to hear.

JANICE. You lied? You lied to me?

SUSIE. No.

JANICE. If it isn't true, it's a lie.

SUSIE. I half-lied.

(Fleeing.)

I mean, it's true that I admire your taste in things, like clothes and furniture, I envy your taste, actually, but I'm just saying I like some of the things I picked out myself.

(Picking up the green swan statue from the liquor cabinet to pack it in the suitcase.)

I like them a lot.

JANICE. Not that? You're not suggesting – you like that piece of –

SUSIE. See, you're just attacking me – you're mocking me and fighting with me, and picking on me and belittling

me and making me feel shitty and if everybody doesn't
stop picking on me – I'll kill myself, goddamnit.

(Rushing off into the bedroom.)

JANICE. Oh, don't start that.

SUSIE. Because I can't stand it.

JANICE. Oh, don't waste your one-size-fits-all manipulations
on me, okay.

(She starts cleaning up, folding clothing.)

SUSIE. *(Offstage.)* Shut up.

JANICE. Because I am not interested in your suicidal razzle
dazzle, all right. I have my own.

*(Coming out of the bedroom, **SUSIE** sits on the
shelf in front of the picture window.)*

SUSIE. But I just never had anything in my entire life,
Janice. I haven't. Growin' up in the desert, for godsake.
I mean, everybody goes to the desert for a vacation, but
I grew up in it. I looked out the window, I saw the sand.
I mean, what do I know about buying furniture or
having a life. My mother liked these lamps with women
on them, their tits lit up when you pulled the switch.
She liked them. And different men, too. We lived way
out in the middle of nowhere. You gotta know what I'm
tryin' to say.

JANICE. *(Pouring a little wine.)* Susie, honey, what I'm
concerned about is that somewhere in that marshmallow
you have for a brain you are hoping to reconcile with
this guy, he might as well be a blunt instrument – I
want to go on record, that if you are thinking of taking
him back, I am no longer available for your goddamn
three a.m. phone calls, I am your nine-one-one, you are
desperate in the middle of the night, you are feeling
anxious, Phil didn't come home, or worse, Phil DID
come home, you are feeling you have lost yourself, you
are feeling empty. Do you know why you are feeling
empty at three a.m., Susie? Because you are empty.
And do you know what else, Susie? Everybody's empty,

Susie. I'm empty. That's the way it is today – people are empty. They don't have anything inside them, and so they eat a lot or drink a lot or watch TV, or they go to church, because everything is outside them. Or better yet, they watch church on TV while they eat and that's best of all – SO GIVE ME A GODDAMN BREAK, SUSIE!

SUSIE. Oh, you're such a snot sometimes, Janice.

(She goes back to packing.)

Do you want me to just casually throw my marriage out the window?

JANICE. Well you better throw your marriage out the window before this guinea from hell throws you out the window.

SUSIE. You know what? I am really getting sick of your so-called jokes at the expense of what is for me my entire little life, okay?

JANICE. Well I'm sick of – what I'm sick of is being over-identified with you. It's ruining my life. I mean, maybe my shrink is right – maybe I really need a break from all this –

SUSIE. Oh, PLEASE, I don't wanna hear about your goddamn shrink again!

JANICE. Why not? Because what Sarah says is that I'm undermining myself just being around you as long as you are in this idiotic marriage with Phil. Because it keeps me trying to work out the way my parents were in this hopeless miserable marriage through –

SUSIE. YOUR PARENTS?! Now we're going to talk about your parents! Gimme a break!

JANICE. No, no, no! I'm talking about you and Phil!

SUSIE. As if I never had to put up with your endless tale of woe from, you know, the land of barbarian surfers.

JANICE. That was a long time ago.

SUSIE. But I put up with it, didn't I – for what seemed like the duration of several boring centuries, when you

were pregnant and Brian of the endless summer had
vanished with some other sun-damaged bimbo

JANICE. You're not comparing Brian and Phil.

SUSIE. No, I'm not. Brian was boring.

JANICE. Brian was gorgeous – he was fascinating and
gorgeous.

SUSIE. He was also made out of the spare parts of some
abandoned space project with a prick for a brain.

JANICE. *(Gathering her purse and bag to leave.)* I mean, the
next time I bore you, Susie, and you don't want to talk
to me about my concerns, please don't humiliate me by
not telling me, okay? Don't undermine my confidence
that way.

SUSIE. But I did talk about you. That's all we did.

JANICE. But you resented it. You resented talking about me
and wanted to be talking about you.

SUSIE. No.

JANICE. That's what you're saying. You don't even know
what you're saying.

SUSIE. I'm talking about now and you're undermining me –
by stealing my undermining idea and saying I'm doing
it to you when you are always undermining me and my
hopes and hurting my feelings.

JANICE. What have I ever done to undermine you?

SUSIE. You have undermined me by undermining me,
that's how you have done it, by just sort of naturally
and thoughtlessly undermining everything I wanted
with Phil, or my desire to have a baby –

JANICE. By offering you some healthy advice?

SUSIE. WHAT healthy advice?

JANICE. *(She marches back to* **SUSIE.***)* Because I mean the
reality is – if you want to know what the reality is – the
reality is, I think, that being in the slightest proximity
to somebody who is actually trying to make some
healthy adjustments in their life is experienced by you
as this overwhelming threat. And so I am experienced

by you as undermining you, for godsake, for suggesting
that you might be a little ungrounded when you are
relating to this semi-professional psychotic who throws
you around the room just to polish his act, but you treat
him as if he has been sent to you by some divinely-
connected Dial-a-Date?! Well, this whole relationship
is exhausting, Susie. It's exhausting. I don't know how
much more I have left for it.

SUSIE. Whata you mean?

JANICE. *(Moving again for the front door.)* I don't know
how much more I have left for you.

SUSIE. I told you we were going to have a fight.

JANICE. No, no, no. It's better that we express these things.

SUSIE. It is not. How is it better? Now we're mad at each
other. How is that better?

JANICE. Well, we know the truth.

SUSIE. I don't.

JANICE. About how we feel.

SUSIE. I don't. We're just mad at each other, that's all I
know. I shouldn't have said what I said and I knew it,
but you made me. You told me you wouldn't get mad at
me and then you did. It wasn't fair.

JANICE. You're right.

SUSIE. That's what you did.

JANICE. But if we don't talk about these things, what would
we talk about?

SUSIE. There's gotta be something else. There's lots of other
things. We could find something.

JANICE. Maybe we shoulda gone somewhere. We coulda
gone out. Maybe we shoulda gone to a movie. You
wanna go to a movie?

> *(She spies the newspaper on the ledge of the
> picture window and starts toward it.)*

SUSIE. *(Collapsing into the swivel chair with the bear.)* I
don't have the strength. I feel like I'm totally made out
of some artificial like tacky material, it has no function,

it was never meant to function. You know, like they've set up this direct line by which to pump toxic waste straight into my heart. How does anybody figure anything out, I wonder.

> (*At the sound of a car outside,* **JANICE** *looks out the window.*)

JANICE. Oh, my god! Phil's coming!

SUSIE. What?

> (*Leaving the bear on the swivel chair, she runs to* **JANICE** *at the window.*)

Oh, god – oh no. Oh, that's our car, there he is!

JANICE. Duck! You can't let him see you, Susie, he's coming. You've got to get out of here!

SUSIE. I didn't even get packed.

> (*Scurrying around, she is grabbing her suitcase, stuffing into it the clothing she can grab.*)

JANICE. Look, just go into the bedroom, and when he comes in, I'll stall him a second, you can get out the back way.

SUSIE. Oh, God, my heart is pounding – it's just pounding.

JANICE. Hurry. Go, go, go.

> (**SUSIE** *goes into bedroom.* **JANICE** *starts toward the kitchen, but* **PHIL** *steps in and she stops.* **PHIL** *is unshaven. He wears the same clothes as before, but they are dirty and wrinkled now. He carries some roses.*)

Hello, Phil. How you doing?

PHIL. Where's Susie?

JANICE. I just come by looking for her.

PHIL. Where is she? Is she here?

> (*He runs to check in the bedroom, and* **JANICE** *moves toward the front door.*)

JANICE. No, no, she's not here, Phil, that's what I'm trying to tell you.

(**PHIL** *sees Susie's scattered clothing; the bear sits on the swivel chair.* **SUSIE** *peeks in the picture window and then flees before he looks back.*)

I was driving by, I thought I'd stop in for a quick cup of coffee but nobody was here. You don't know where she is? Where you been Phil?

PHIL. I had some auditions, so I been out. Why do you ask?

JANICE. She told me you guys had a terrible fight.

PHIL. You're a piece'a work, Janice.

JANICE. She said it was a really big one.

PHIL. I just come to get some clean socks and stuff, I know she don't want me here until after we talk. You tell her that, though. You tell her that I gotta talk to her.

JANICE. I don't know if I'll hear from her but I'll give her the message if I do.

PHIL. Right. Of course. How else? Maybe I'll just write her a note.

(**PHIL** *goes to telephone table where he finds a tablet and a pen.*)

JANICE. Sure, that's a good idea. Bye bye.

(*She goes, and* **PHIL** *pushes the button and his messages start to play as he leans against the couch and begins writing a note to Susie. Behind him, the closet door opens and* **SAL** *steps out, holding his stomach. He's disheveled, his coat maybe off, his tie loose. He steps to the couch and as he leans over, sick to his stomach, he groans and* **PHIL** *whirls, seeing him.*)

PHIL. Jesus Christ! Where the hell did you come from?

SAL. Look, I ain't feelin' so good. I just been through a horrible experience, okay.

(**SAL** *heads toward the bathroom.*)

PHIL. I can't get it outa my mind you have come to town to hurt me, and if that's what you wanta do, now is the time, because I am numb at this particular juncture.

(*He turns off the answering machine.*)

SAL. I have just had the most terrible experience of my life and in it I was without the opportunity to pee. I gotta pee. Ohh, my stomach is carryin' on like I swallowed one a them roto-rooters.

(*Stepping into the bathroom.*)

PHIL. So what was this horrible experience? This was with that Hollywood lowlife?

(*He keeps writing his note.*)

SAL. (*Offstage.*) Mort? You talkin' about Mort? How could that be horrible? I mean, this guy is a pony ride. He's one of these ponies, they go around in circles, little boys and girls fuck with them.

(*Coming out of the bathroom, bringing aftershave lotion, he freshens up at the mirror.*)

So he's at this restaurant and after awhile I hear how he likes to talk about things, they are the bottom line. I am at a nearby table, so in the parking lot, I introduce myself. "We have mutual friends in Vegas, Mort," I tell him, "I am the bottom line." He looks at me and shits his pants. Whata stink. Don't beg, Phil. Don't ever beg.

PHIL. I know that.

(*Moving to the swivel chair, he puts the roses and the note with the bear.*)

SAL. It don't work. It don't fuckin' ever work.

PHIL. So where's Mort now – I mean, after he changed his underwear.

SAL. I would guess he's crackin' open his kids' piggy banks and beggin' his lowlife friends for the necessary funds to get him out from under.

PHIL. I wanna get outa here. If you're done pampering and coiffing yourself. Let's go.

> (**PHIL** *crosses to the front door.*)

SAL. Why do you wanna get out of here? Where would we go? I like it here. Let's have a drink. C'mon, one drink.

> (**SAL** *goes to the refrigerator for ice.*)

PHIL. Okay, but just one. I feel like shit.

SAL. You look like shit, you know. You got rings around your eyes, Phil, your clothes are all wrinkled – this is terrible.

> (*At the liquor cabinet, he pours a couple of drinks.*)

PHIL. We had a fight – Susie and me – it started little, so it got big – she threw me out. Now I wanna come back. You know how that goes. But I don't want her thinking I have like tried to sneak up on her and catch her off guard. I call ahead and then I come by.

SAL. You're a gentlemen.

> (*As he brings the drink to* **PHIL.**)

PHIL. What would you do?

SAL. As myself?

PHIL. Whatayamean?

SAL. As myself? What would I do as myself, or if like you, I had become a pathetic piece of shit – what would I do?

PHIL. Relent, I beg you.

SAL. I'm sorry if I offend you, I am just trying to answer your question. Salud.

> (**SAL** *raises his glass.*)

PHIL. (*Gulps his drink and moves again to front door.*) All right, now, let's get outa here.

SAL. I can't go out with you lookin' like you do. You look like you're a fuckin' homeless. Put on a suit.

> (**SAL** *crosses up to the closet.*)

PHIL. I wanna go.

SAL. *(From the closet, he pulls out the suit he found earlier.)* Put on a suit, and we'll go. I remember this suit.

PHIL. Where'd you get that? You been burglarizin' my house, Sal?

SAL. Just put it on. I can't stand the sight of you.

PHIL. Then we go to a bar. We go to a bar and get smashed.

SAL. Is that what you wanna do? You wanna go to a bar and get smashed? Why don't we get smashed here? Or is it that you are worried that this ball-buster of a wife might come back, and so you are worried that she might find you relaxing in your own goddamn house. Who pays the rent?

　　　*(As **PHIL** moves in and grabs the suit.)*

PHIL. Fuck you.

　　　(He strides up toward the mirror to start to dress.)

SAL. *(Prowling over to the swivel chair, he examines the note, the flowers, the bear.)* This is like that old guy – what was his name? – twenty years back, I can't remember it – he was a stone killer, whata load a balls he had – there were occasional contracts put out on him but only the loonies would think to take them because the sane people did not believe that if you shot this guy he would actually die. But there was this broad and he could not get away from her – and she would degrade him and humiliate him and god as my witness, the only thing he would come back begging for was more. How does this happen to a man, Phil?

PHIL. How do I know?

SAL. *(Moving up to stand behind **PHIL**, who looks in the mirror.)* Whata you think, though? Nobody knows. Take a guess. I don't mean to embarrass you but it's unavoidable.

PHIL. Why are you here? WHY THE FUCK ARE YOU HERE?

SAL. I DON'T KNOW WHY I'M HERE! We're all just here. People are here. That's the way things are now. So they

do things. Things happen. Somebody wants somethin'
– they talk to me – then what? Ideas are exchanged.
This guy's got ideas, he gives them to me – some other
guy has given them to him. Thereafter, I have these two
other guys' ideas.

> *(Back at the liquor cabinet he pours another
> drink for* **PHIL.***)*

I don't know why I'm here. Except to make us another
drink and ask you how does this happen to a man,
Phil? You shoulda knocked her on her ass.

PHIL. That's the trouble. I did.

SAL. You did?

> *(Clinking the two drinks together, he heads
> back to* **PHIL.***)*

Good!

PHIL. No, it ain't good, Sal. She's my wife. I love her.

> *(Taking the drink,* **PHIL** *goes back to dressing
> as the sun sets and the rooms darkens.)*

SAL. You love her.

PHIL. You wanna humiliate me, I don't care. I love her.

SAL. Don't get me wrong. I'm just tryin' to understand.

PHIL. I go crazy sometimes. What I shouldn't do, that's
exactly what I devote myself one hundred percent to I
GOTTA DO IT.

SAL. So did she hurt your feelings or what?

PHIL. No!

SAL. She didn't hurt your feelings.

PHIL. No.

SAL. With all due respect to you, Phil, I gotta tell you or
I would be dishonoring what is to me an important
thing and by that I mean our friendship, but you are a
fucking liar.

PHIL. Yeh?

SAL. Yeh. They do somethin' – they always do somethin' but
it's not what a man would do, so you are not prepared

to see it. How do they do it? That's what I want to know. Like that goddamn Charlene – you remember her? I know you do.

PHIL. Oh, she was gorgeous, Sal – I'm not gonna forget Charlene!

(Still changing shirt, suit, shoes.)

SAL. I threw up over her, Phil. We were babies, twelve, thirteen, right? Little babies. I puked my guts out. First when she says she WOULD go out with me. I hadda run around the corner where I upchucked everything but my shoes. So we go to a movie and she fucks me on the very first date down in her uncle's basement. It was unbelievable. So the next day, she blows me. I'm like this kid at a carnival ride, I don't know what's gonna happen next. So then she dumps me and I start pukin' – like my heart had tore loose inside me and it was comin' up with the chunks a beef stew and the rest of the puke. What does Susie do to you?

*(**PHIL** is now in the dark suit, tie, and shoes.)*

PHIL. She don't do nothin'.

SAL. What does she do?

PHIL. I think I had a nightmare recently, Sal – and you were in it.

SAL. Good.

PHIL. How do they do it? You want to know how they do it? They make this fuckin' promise to you, broads, is what they do – they make this promise, but they do not keep it.

(Grabbing his drink, he leans against the shelf in front of the window.)

Does this sound familiar?

SAL. Of course.

*(He leans to drink with **PHIL**.)*

PHIL. They are these shylocks, and they offer to give you something, I don't wanna call it happiness, because it's worse than happiness, but you want it; and then when they own you completely, they call the whole thing back. Let's face it – you're right – Susie looks at me sometimes, I feel like I am a dog, I been hit by a car – I wanna run around and hide with my tail between my legs.

(Moving to the liquor cabinet.)

SAL. That's their racket.

PHIL. LET'S FACE IT – YOU'RE RIGHT. Somehow they do it, they do it all under the table, they can throw this scare into you – you don't see it comin'!

SAL. She threw you outa your own house. Fuck her.

PHIL. *(At the swivel chair, tossing the roses and the bear to the floor.)* You couldn't be more right than that you are saying that.

SAL. I was fucking this broad, and she says to me, "Wear your gun," and she meant the holster and everything. They think they can get on like a tour bus through the underworld, they will go sightseeing. Whatsamatter with any of them? Have you asked yourself that?

PHIL. Yes. And I have answered – I DON'T KNOW!

(Crumpling and tossing the note.)

I DO NOT KNOW! This is however, my verdict –

SAL. What?

PHIL. I get a few in me and I figure, it's all a lot of shit, I might a well be dead, but then again, I'm not. Let's put on some music.

SAL. Like Charlene. She was the first and last. From her on, if anybody pukes, it's THEM. How come you wanna put on any music?

PHIL. I don't know. Let's dance.

SAL. Whata you mean?

PHIL. I feel like that's what you come here to do – all this way from wherever. To dance. And we been dancin' for a while now. Don't you wanna dance with me, Sal?

SAL. Maybe. What would be the music?

PHIL. Anything you want. You tell me. Maybe Francis Albert.

SAL. No, no, it ain't him I'm thinkin' about.

PHIL. Who are you thinkin' about?

SAL. It's somethin' particular and like from far back and I can feel the feelings the tune would make me feel and it's sad, but I can't think what it is.

PHIL. But you heard it.

SAL. We both heard it. We was in a bar.

PHIL. We been in a lotta bars, Sal. This is aggravating, Sal. Why you always gotta start with this aggravating shit?

> *(Distracted by a framed photograph nearby, he picks it up.)*

You see this? You remember her, my big sister, Angelina? And she was an angel, too. I didn't know you when my dad run out on me, did I.

SAL. No. Who knows where I was?

PHIL. So then my mom run out on us. There was my brother, Joey, who went to work, and Angelina – she's dead now. She was an angel, too. I was just a baby. The nuns took this in the eighth grade. They liked her. Everybody liked her.

> *(**SAL** takes the picture and lays down on the couch, his head toward center stage. **PHIL** kneels behind the couch, looking at the picture **SAL** holds.)*

SAL. I thought when I first met you she was your mother.

PHIL. Do you know what I think?

SAL. What?

PHIL. When we go after some broad, I mean some one particular broad – and I'm not just talkin' pussy here so this is an important distinction – I want you to keep it in mind – but what I'm talkin' about is we go after one particular broad, what are we doin'?

SAL. I have no idea.

PHIL. What do we think we're gonna get? So what is it? Is it love? Do you think that's right?

SAL. I don't know.

PHIL. So if we are...

SAL. Yeh.

PHIL. And then one of them takes up with us, do you know what I think? They're doin' the same thing. That's what they are doin', too. They are looking for love, too.

SAL. No.

PHIL. I think so, Sal.

SAL. No.

PHIL. So then you got it in which I am lookin' for it in her, and she is lookin' for it in me, and do you know what that means? Neither one of us got any is what it means, and so there ain't any. There is zero love in such a goddamn situation.

SAL. You don't really think that's what they're doin' do you?

PHIL. So you got two people neither one of 'em got any, both of 'em lookin' for it like a couple a rats in the garbage.

SAL. That they could be doin' that, that they could be so stupid as to be lookin' for that in somethin' like a man. That never dawned on me.

PHIL. *(Taking the picture he returns it to the shelf.)* I think that's what's goin' on.

SAL. I'm tryin' to imagine some broad she's lookin' for love in me. I mean, "I don't know, I lost it at the track. It's in my other suit at the cleaners."

> *(Taking a pillow from the couch,* **PHIL** *moves to the windowsill. The moon is unnaturally huge outside the window.)*

PHIL. So you got two people lookin' for it, neither one got it – two starvin' rats in the garbage and you call it your marriage.

> *(***PHIL** *lays down on the shelf unit, stretched out along the window.)*

SAL. Did you have any starvin' rats in your building when you were a kid?

PHIL. Of course.

SAL. They make a lot a fuckin' noise. I used to hunt them with this fishin' pole. You could hook 'em with cheese. And then, I would hang him out the window on the eleventh floor, so if they got off or if they didn't, they were dead either way, wigglin' and squealin'.

> (*PHIL and* SAL *are stretched out in their suits, one on the shelf, the other on the couch, like bodies laid out in a funeral home, their heads in opposite directions.*)

PHIL. Do you know what I think will be the next ice age, Sal?

SAL. Whata you mean?

PHIL. You remember when we would worry, you know, we was just little kids at night, little kids sittin' on the stoop at night and we was worried – what would be the next ice age?

SAL. Yeh.

PHIL. And we would think, would it be earthquakes or flood? Or like this other earlier awful ice age by which everything in the world was brought to an end?

SAL. Yeh.

PHIL. Do you know what? We are the fucking ice age. Us. People. We're the terrible thing that's come to leave the world a wreck, and we're here now. People. We've arrived.

SAL. That's an interesting thought, Phil. You mean the whole world, not just our world, but the outside world, the big world, the world world.

PHIL. That's what I mean.

> (*For a beat they are quiet.*)

SAL. (*Sleepily.*) Do you know what, Phil?

PHIL. (*Almost asleep.*) What?

SAL. This ain't what we was talkin' about. What was we talkin' about?

PHIL. (*Very sleepy.*) When?

SAL. Before. We were talkin' about somethin' else.

PHIL. Right. What was it?

SAL. We couldn't remember it.

PHIL. We still can't.

SAL. Dancin'.

PHIL. Right. The song.

SAL. It was that kid.

PHIL. What kid?

SAL. That kid we took fishing. There was this stewardess, right? He come back from the jukebox – he had her, he's so hot for her his balls are blue. You remember him.

PHIL. He thinks he loves her, sure.

SAL. It was their song, he says. But I can't remember it.

PHIL. What was it?

SAL. I can hear it in my head. I can see him walkin' back.

PHIL. What about a lyric? That way we could track it down.

SAL. I'm drawin' a blank. Just the tune. Sad, you know. But it was doo-wop.

PHIL. It was doo-wop?

SAL. Yeh, yeh.

> (**SAL** *moves to the liquor for a refill, as* **PHIL** *heads to the stereo.*)

PHIL. That's a hint. But there's a lot of doo-wop.

> (*Rooting in the records.*)

I got a lot of 'em here.

> (*He puts a record on.*)

SAL. I did my best. But at least we know it was doo-wop. At least we know there was a bar and music.

> (*Music starts: a slow doo-wop, soft beat, sad woman's voice.**)

---

*A license to produce *Those the River Keeps* does not include a performance license for any third-party or copyrighted music. Licensees should create an original composition or use music in the public domain. For further information, please see Music Use Note on page 3.

PHIL. So we gonna dance or not? You says we were gonna dance.

SAL. Sure.

> (**SAL** *empties the glass, then faces* **PHIL**, *who is moving down from the window, dancing.*)

You remember that kid. He come back, his brain long lost in the carnival ride he imagined to exist between that stewardess's legs. You remember. He was hopin' the music might make her gamey.

PHIL. That's the kid you been talkin' about.

SAL. Right. The one you took out, Phil. Him.

PHIL. I never took no kid out.

> (**PHIL** *moves to the music as* **SAL** *starts toward him.*)

SAL. Phil, please – let's face it – you did. I know you says the other day you didn't, but you did. Lie to yourself if you want to. I don't care about that. Phil is lyin' to me, I said. He's tryin' to take advantage of my pathetic memory and make out our lives were different than they were. So then I thought you musta laid it off on me. That was what you done at your table with Arthur and Big Tommy, you laid that kid off on me. What'd you tell 'em, you was drunk, you wasn't even there? Who cares? But you took your gun, you put it behind his ear.

> (*With only a few feet between them.*)

I was with you, Phil. We were young together.

> (*He opens his arms in welcome.*)

PHIL. (*Struggling for a beat, he moves to* **SAL** *and they begin to dance.*) And then we burned the car.

SAL. You couldn't forget that, how could you?

PHIL. The upholstery was plastic and there was these little doodads, they all melted and gave off some terrible smell. It was this awful plastic stink.

SAL. So why did we want to burn the car?

PHIL. I don't think we wanted to, I think we just did it.

SAL. Why?

PHIL. I think we were like bystanders, you know, amazed that it had happened.

SAL. It was just there before us, this burnin' car.

PHIL. And Bobby was in the river, in there with the fish.

SAL. Bobbi was the girl.

PHIL. No. No, Jeananne was the girl – she was from like Ohio.

SAL. Right. You're right.

PHIL. I know I'm right. That's what I said it for. Jeananne was the girl.

> *(Having danced across the stage with* **SAL** *moving backward, they pause, then start back the other way.)*

SAL. Your wife, Phil, is a terrible bitch and you should know it. Your marriage is over, thank god.

PHIL. What?

SAL. She was talkin', Phil – it was horrible – she was talkin'!

PHIL. This was horrible – she was talkin'?

SAL. Inna restaurant. To this other awful broad – this Janice! This disgrace of a life you been livin', you can't live it anymore.

PHIL. What the fuck are you getting at?

SAL. God forbid, it was you, they were talkin' about. It made me sick. What did you do to piss this Janice off so terrible, Phil?

PHIL. Janice hates me. She's always hated me. What was she sayin'?

SAL. No, no, please. Have some mercy. It was hard enough I hadda hear it, let alone you are gonna coerce me I gotta repeat it.

PHIL. Don't torment me here, Sal! I wanna know! What was she sayin'?

SAL. I mean, it wasn't just her, and it went on and on and on – it was like a couple a guys, they are torturing some creep, for whom they are filled with loathing, so now it's a contest about who can come up with the most vicious thing anybody can think of.

PHIL. Susie was in on it, too? She was doin' it, too?

SAL. It was a feeding frenzy – it was degenerate and degrading and –

PHIL. Gimme one example. I want to hear one example.

SAL. It was insults, Phil – if one of 'em puts a knife in your eye, the other's gotta rip off your balls.

PHIL. Specifically, goddamnit! I wanna hear the specifics.

SAL. She's done with you.

PHIL. Yeh.

SAL. The marriage is over.

PHIL. I can talk her outa that. What else?

SAL. Why would you want to talk her out of that?

PHIL. I can change her mind on that.

SAL. And the other one, this Janice, calls you a guinea, and Susie's gonna bust a gut she's laughin' so hard, and she can't wait, she says, to get away, 'cause you're stupid, and there's some really mean, nasty shit about your nose – really mean, nasty –

PHIL. They were bad-mouthing my nose?

SAL. Yeh.

PHIL. I don't understand that. They were insulting my nose?

SAL. Who could understand it? It's so awful, she can't wait to get away so she can get it on with some guy he's younger, he's one a these surfer creeps, a nautilus freak, he's young, he's blonde, he can fuck, he can talk about the beach –

> *(The dance movements have reflected their struggle. But now **PHIL** breaks free, rushing to the record player.)*

PHIL. WAIT A MINUTE! WAIT A FUCKIN' MINUTE!

SAL. That's what she says! They're goin' on and on about these guys and their suntan –

PHIL. *(Shutting off the music.)* WHAT GUYS?

SAL. These guys, these surfer guys, they pump the weights before they pump each other.

PHIL. Did he have a name?

SAL. The guy?

PHIL. The surfer guy! DID HE HAVE A FUCKIN' NAME?!

SAL. We can find him! I can find him! We can get him!

PHIL. This is what she does to me – I think everything is okay, I trust her, I wanna make things work – the next thing I know I'm walkin' around, she has covered me in shit!

> (*Despairing,* **PHIL** *flops down in the swivel chair.*)

SAL. Listen to me, Phil – there are people in the East – you can remember it – you gotta try, you are remembered there – people would welcome you.

PHIL. Where was this restaurant?

> (*Heading for the front door.*)

SAL. What?

PHIL. This restaurant where she was! I wanna see her.

SAL. It was hours ago, Phil. They wouldn't be there.

PHIL. Right. She's probably at Janice's.

> (*Darting to the phone.*)

SAL. Whata you doin'?

PHIL. I'm gonna call her! I gotta talk to her.

> (*He heads to the kitchen table, throwing on the light and sitting at the table to dial.*)

SAL. Look. She's a terrible evil bitch. Forget about her.

> (*Grabbing the phone away.*)

PHIL. I can't. I go nuts, thinkin' about her and these other guys, Sal, even these surfer assholes. It's like Charlene – you remember – it's –

SAL. (*Grabbing a beer from the fridge.*) That was three million years ago! I was a baby! Are you a baby! Have a drink.

(He guides the beer to **PHIL**'s *mouth again and again.)*

Have another one, have another big swig, a big one – take another one. Now listen to me.

(He sits across the table from **PHIL**.*)*

Listen to me!

PHIL. I have been known to follow her around sometimes just to watch her – just to see her do the stuff she does, you know, she's shoppin', or whatever, I like to watch her. I love her, Sal. What am I gonna do?

SAL. She's your wife.

PHIL. It's sick, I know – I'm a pussy in this area, I know it. It's disgusting, forgive me – I can't help myself – you have every right, you have every right, but it's like she's got my heart, see, and it's gone from inside me, she's reached inside me somehow and she got it, and she's got it in her hands, and it ain't a big heart, it's a little heart, like somethin' like an egg, and she can do with it whatever she wants.

SAL. You don't want her foolin' around with these other guys. Of course not.

PHIL. I'd rather she's dead than she's goin' off with these other guys! I can't bear it!

(Reaching for the phone.)

SAL. *(Stopping him.)* But I can fix it if that's what you're worryin' about. I can take care of this guy – just tell me who he is. I'll find him, I can fix him for you. This Janice – where does she live, where does she eat? Just tell me. Who am I? I don't even exist out here. Planes. Cars. I'm here, I ain't here. I'm like the wind. What am I? I blow through. Some things get blown away. That's all, that's the way it is with guys like us. We're just the wind. Gimme a couple hours. You won't have to worry about your wife anymore – what is she doing? Who is she with? And Janice – she gets to meet the real guinea from Mars, she gets to see the real dago from hell.

PHIL. Whata you talkin' about?

SAL. That's what she called you. Why should she be around to torment you? I agree. Fuck her.

PHIL. You're gonna hit my wife? Is that what you're sayin'? You'll take her out?

SAL. I'll do it for you. You don't even have to know, Phil. Don't concern yourself. I can be like a ghost. I can float in the alleys and be like the dog on their trail. I love it. "Who's that?" they say. "I don't know him." Then it's over.

PHIL. Sal, wait a minute.

SAL. That's right. It's over. All of it. Think about it. The old ways are the best ways. You know that. This Janice, she deserves it. You know she does. I'll finish up with the Hollywood douchebag, and then I'll go visit the girls.

PHIL. *(He indicates the front door.)* Sal, I want you out of my house. I want you out of here.

SAL. What are you talkin' about?

>   *(Heading to the front door, which he flings open.)*

PHIL. I want you outa my house. You should walk out the door.

>   *(Throwing on a nearby light switch.)*

SAL. Whatsamatter with you now?

PHIL. You're a degenerate. I don't want you here.

SAL. I DON'T KNOW WHAT YOU MEAN!

PHIL. Get out.

SAL. Why are you trying to hurt my feelings?

PHIL. You don't understand I say you should get outa my house? It means you should get outa my house, you should walk out the door – that's what it means.

>   *(A bottle sits on the window shelves, the bottle* **SAL** *placed there on his way out in Act I, and* **PHIL** *grabs it and takes a big drink.)*

SAL. But I wanna talk to you. How am I gonna talk to you if I leave your house?

PHIL. DON'T YOU HURT HER. DON'T YOU HURT SUSIE.

SAL. Okay, so I won't.

PHIL. *(Moving back toward* **SAL**.*)* You understand, that is not a possibility!

SAL. Absolutely.

PHIL. You disgust me, you talk like that.

SAL. Of course. I disgust myself!

PHIL. I don't understand you.

SAL. I DON'T UNDERSTAND YOU! You gotta condemn me on accounta I thought of something. Big deal. A person thinks about everything.

PHIL. But you said it.

SAL. You said it!

PHIL. I did not.

SAL. We was right here.

> *(Rising suddenly, moving for the door.)*

I'm gonna go.

PHIL. Where you goin', Sal?

> *(***PHIL** *scoots to get between* **SAL** *and the door.)*

SAL. Whata you care? You don't like me.

PHIL. I care that you understand me! I care about that! You understand what I'm sayin'?

SAL. I hear what you're sayin' but I also know what you're thinkin'.

PHIL. Just listen to me, goddamnit!

SAL. *(Turning to face* **PHIL** *at the door.)* I KNOW WHAT YOU ARE GONNA SAY – She's hurt you and she hurt you bad and you do not want her occupying the same earth as you anymore, you do not want her inhabiting this present current period of time and space with you which we are now in!

PHIL. WHAT THE HELL IS WRONG WITH YOU?

SAL. Nothin'. I said I ain't gonna do it!

PHIL. You think that's what I want, though? You think that's what I want?

SAL. I'm goin'. I'm gettin' out of your house, like you told me. That's all I'm doin'.

> (**SAL** *turns to step out the door and* **PHIL** *whacks him in the back of the head with the bottle.*)

Owww owwww owwww owwww.

PHIL. That's what I want! THAT'S WHAT I WANT!

> (**SAL** *drops to the floor, out cold, as* **PHIL** *pulls a handgun from a holster on* **SAL**'*s leg and jumps back.* **SAL** *bolts awake, flailing, rolling.*)

You stay there. You stay there you sonofabitch. Or I'm gonna give you three in the head, you prick, do you understand me?

SAL. *(Sitting up, waking up, having ended up downstage.)* What's goin' on? I'm bleedin' here, you crazy prick, have you lost your mind?

PHIL. Do you want to die?

SAL. I want to be on your side, Phil. How can you not see that –

PHIL. THEN SHUT UP! Or I'll give it to you in the ear! Do you want it in the ear?

> (**PHIL** *jams the gun in* **SAL**'*s ear.*)

SAL. No.

PHIL. Huh? The eye, huh?

SAL. No.

PHIL. The cranium.

SAL. Where?

PHIL. There!

> (*Jamming the gun against the back of* **SAL**'*s head.*)

You jackass!

SAL. No.

PHIL. Up the ass?

SAL. No. I don't.

PHIL. Shut up.

SAL. What'd I do, Phil? What'd I do?

PHIL. I mean this as a friend, Sal. You ain't had your batteries changed for a long long time, Sal!

SAL. Of course. I know that.

PHIL. YOU'RE DEPRESSIN' ME, SAL.

SAL. This ain't good Phil – that we are at each other's throats.

PHIL. For days, I was drivin' and drivin' and I had the heebie-jeebies but I did not know what I had the heebie-jeebies about. I could put a slug in you, and it would all be over. My life, it would be over.

SAL. Yeh? How?

PHIL. I would have killed you! There is this line...and on one side, I am me and on that other side I am somethin' else and I mean, I shoot you, but my life – MY LIFE – is over.

SAL. What about me?

PHIL. WHO GIVES A FUCK ABOUT YOU? I don't care about you. Nobody cares about you.

SAL. Right. You're right. But I ain't gonna beg. Could I have a towel? I'm makin' a fuckin' mess, here.

PHIL. Don't try nothin'.

> (*Backing into the kitchen,* **PHIL** *grabs a towel and throws it to* **SAL.** **PHIL** *sits down in the kitchen, watching* **SAL.**)

SAL. What am I gonna try? You got me.

> (*Wiping the blood with the towel.*)

You know – it was weird, but just before you gimme a smack with that bottle, I had this premonition – I says, "Phil is gonna hit me with a bottle, I wonder why." Whata you make a that?

PHIL. Nothin'.

SAL. I thought maybe it was religious.

PHIL. I doubt it.

SAL. Probably not.

PHIL. I mean, you got to figure...

> *(He turns out the kitchen light.)*

...there's the bullshit factor and there's the lunatic factor, there's what everybody knows and there's what nobody knows...

> *(He turns out the lamp on the phone table.)*

...and there's this thing called luck and this thing called fate...

> *(He throws the switch by the front door, checks outside, and then shuts the front door.)*

...and there's these things that people call them good and bad and any of them they could be a factor, good or bad or fate – in any moment of your life, they could be a factor, and you ask yourself, "Which is it at this particular moment like now?" And you must answer, "I do not know. Phil does not know. Does Sal know?"

SAL. No, I don't.

PHIL. What was you doin' when you was talkin' about the wind, you was callin' yourself the wind – why did you do that?

SAL. I don't remember doin' it. Are you drunk, Phil?

PHIL. Of course.

> *(Advancing on **SAL**, he picks up the teddy bear.)*

SAL. I am drunk, too. It's always your best friend ain't it – it's always your best friend is the one they get to take you out.

> *(On his hands and knees, as **PHIL** aims at the back of **SAL**'s head.)*

I wish you wouldn't. But on the other hand, it has been a long life.

*(As **PHIL** wraps the bear on the barrel as a kind of silencer.)*

SAL. Are there any convenient rivers in California?

PHIL. No. But there is the ocean.

SAL. The ocean? The fucking ocean? Are you serious? Can you imagine that?

*(**PHIL** cocks the hammer.)*

Can I tell you something, Phil?

PHIL. What?

SAL. You're gonna make a terrible mess. You should put down a blanket underneath me, or you're gonna have my brains all over the rug here, your wife will be pissed at you.

PHIL. My wife. You ain't ever gonna let it alone about my wife, are you?!

SAL. I could. Sure.

PHIL. But you ain't gonna. You ain't ever gonna!

*(**PHIL** storms to get blanket from closet. He hurls it at **SAL** and sits on the couch.)*

I don't know what I'm gonna do with you, Sal. I feel like you're gonna hold a grudge against me; you're gonna want revenge.

SAL. We shoulda called up some girls, Phil – one a them Escort Services. You know the number for one of them, they are around here?

(On the floor, he leans against the armchair, covering himself with the blanket, making a nest.)

PHIL. They're in the yellow pages, Sal.

SAL. We shoulda done that.

(As he draws the teddy bear into his nest.)

That way we coulda avoided this whole thing here. But its too late now. I don't feel like it anyway. I got blood all over my shirt. Who would wanna fuck me?

(Lying on his back, he has the bear set over his crotch.)

Is this a boy bear or a girl bear?

PHIL. Don't get randy with the bear, Sal.

SAL. What kind of bear is this?

PHIL. Don't get randy with the bear Sal. Damnit, or I will shoot you in the head.

SAL. For god's sake Phil, is everything I do wrong in your eyes?

PHIL. That's a bear, he is blissfully ignorant of the things of our world.

SAL. I know that. Anybody could see that.

(Studying the bear.)

You can see it in the shininess of his eyes. He got shiny eyes. I'm feelin' very strange here, very unnatural. You hit me hard, Phil. You hit me in the back of the head where, as we all know, we are vulnerable. I was out. The lights went out.

PHIL. You wasn't out long.

SAL. I saw stuff. It was quick. But I saw stuff.

PHIL. What kinda stuff?

SAL. Dead people. Dead people who weren't dead.

PHIL. Cut the crap.

SAL. No, I did. I saw 'em. I'm feelin' very unlike myself. I went somewhere.

PHIL. Bullshit.

SAL. No. I did. I went and I come back, I think. Maybe I was one of those near-death people.

PHIL. You was right here, Sal. I hit you, you fell. You never went anywhere. I kept my eye on you. You never went anywhere.

SAL. I'm tellin' you, I was lookin' at the river – leanin' over a fence and lookin' at the water, and then I was seein' all the way into the water and down to the bottom. And they were all there. Everybody.

PHIL. Who?

SAL. The dead. You were there. We were together. We were all there.

PHIL. I was dead? I ain't dead. Were you dead?

SAL. It must be we made a mistake. Somebody says they'll give us a ride, so we get in the car, and that's our one mistake which once we have made it, we don't get a second chance.

PHIL. I ain't dead.

SAL. But that's the thing, Phil. That's what I saw. Everybody of any worth – they are the dead. Fuck the living, who cares about them. It's good to be dead.

(**PHIL** *sits on the coffee table.*)

It was like from – if I had one – my soul, and I come back to tell you. So our guts are cut open, whata mess – and we're sinkin' – we have made our mistake, and the water's gray – and then we get to the bottom, and there everybody is, all the ones who never came up, the kids there, and Big Tommy. And Jeananne's there. And you and me – our bellies all slit – and your miserable dad, and your asshole mom, and my uncle Alphonse, who kicked the crap out of me if he saw me, he's there. All the ones the water will not let back up, and so we are the ones kept by the river.

(*On his feet now,* **SAL** *looks down on* **PHIL** *seated on the coffee table.*)

PHIL. I wanted to be a good person, Sal. That's what I wanted.

SAL. You are a good person, Phil.

PHIL. No. I ain't.

SAL. Sure. I think you are.

PHIL. I'm somebody who wants to be good but he ain't. I mean, a regular person, Sal; he comes home, he watches the television, he has a wife and kids. That was my idea, but now I feel that you have come, and I have got to say goodbye to all hope for anything but the terrible things you offer, I got to be like you and say goodbye to decency and little houses and goodbye to smiles and clean faces.

SAL. Maybe I should go.

PHIL. Maybe.

SAL. I think I will.

(He steps toward the door with PHIL watching closely.)

PHIL. You know what? I'm gonna keep the gun.

SAL. Sure. I got more. We walked into somethin' here – what was it?

PHIL. Things got wild.

SAL. My personal feeling is we got plastered, you know, and when that happens, anything is the result. But all those things you were talkin' about, goodbye, goodbye, goodbye, I never thought about them.

(By the door, he turns and faces PHIL.)

I just missed you. I wanted to help you. You hit me with a fuckin' bottle – so that's the question now – am I gonna be big enough to forget about it? And do you know what? Yes, I am.

PHIL. So you're gonna be my rabbi now, huh, Sal? You're gonna be my priest.

SAL. Of course. I bless you, too. Feel better.

(He blesses PHIL.)

PHIL. This is what I get – you're the devil and the devil loves me.

SAL. There was always somethin' about you – you thought you was different. But you ain't so different. I'll be back for you, Phil. Isn't that the way it is with people they have their loyalties. That's what we would say when we were kids and we were goin' somewhere and one of us couldn't go when it was time to go. Now I'm goin' and you can't just now. So "I'll be back for you, Phil." You gonna shoot me before I get out the door?

PHIL. We'll see.

SAL. Right. We'll see.

> (*Music.** **SAL** *stands near the door.* **PHIL** *stands, watching.*)
>
> (*Blackout.*)

---

*A license to produce *Those the River Keeps* does not include a performance license for any third-party or copyrighted music. Licensees should create an original composition or use music in the public domain. For further information, please see Music Use Note on page 3.

Scene Two

(Music. Lights slowly find **PHIL** in the dark in the swivel chair, his tie undone, suit open. He has the bear and the handgun. The blanket, roses, and crumpled note lie on the floor. The door opens and **SUSIE** comes in, startling him. He places the gun in a way that the chair blocks it from her view. She wears a white flare dress, buttons down the front, thin straps over her bare shoulders. She wears high heels and carries her suitcase. As the music fades out, she throws the light switch on and sees him.)*

SUSIE. Oh. Phil.

PHIL. Susie. You surprised me. Sorry.

SUSIE. What are you doing? You got the bear.

PHIL. Oh, yeh. Well, I was just looking at him. I don't know – he was here, you know.

SUSIE. Why were you looking at him?

PHIL. Well – what do you mean?

SAL. You were looking at him – and I wanted to know why.

PHIL. I don't think I have any idea, you know. He was just there and I picked him up. I don't know if I had a reason.

SUSIE. Oh.

PHIL. You know. Maybe I did. Don't you want me to have him?

SUSIE. No, I don't mind, as long as you're nice to him. There's no reason to be mean to him.

PHIL. Oh, no, no. I wasn't bein' mean to him.

---

*A license to produce *Those the River Keeps* does not include a performance license for any third-party or copyrighted music. Licensees should create an original composition or use music in the public domain. For further information, please see Music Use Note on page 3.

(He hides the gun in the blanket beneath the chair.)

PHIL. I was being nice to him. I think I was just, you know, looking at him. He's okay. So how are you, Susie? You okay?

SUSIE. Oh, sure.

PHIL. Good.

*(**SUSIE** moves to the kitchen, setting down her suitcase.)*

SUSIE. Why?

PHIL. I was just wondering. You know. You been with Janice?

SUSIE. *(Taking a club soda from the fridge.)* We had a fight.

PHIL. Oh, you did? You and Janice? You had a fight?

SUSIE. Yes.

PHIL. That's too bad, I guess.

SUSIE. I've been miserable, Phil, if you want to know in actuality – I have not been okay.

(Sitting at the kitchen table.)

PHIL. Oh, I'm sorry to hear that. Was it a bad fight, I guess, a big fight?

SUSIE. I have been very miserable about us, Phil. About you and me. Because I just feel we have no choice but we have to get a divorce.

PHIL. Oh, no. Is that what you think? Because I don't. I really don't.

SUSIE. Well, I do.

PHIL. But if it makes you miserable? I mean, if it makes you miserable, why even –

SUSIE. Can I have the bear?

PHIL. The bear?

SUSIE. Can I have him?

PHIL. Of course. Of course.

(Delivering the bear, he hovers in the kitchen.)

Because, see, Susie, the thing I was getting at is I have come to the opposite conclusion on the exact same issue. You have come to one conclusion, but I have come to the totally, exact opposite.

SUSIE. And what's that? That you love me? You can't live without me, like you been leavin' in all my messages? Huh? Is that what it is?

PHIL. *(Stymied, because that was pretty much it.)* Well...

(He spots the flowers under the swivel chair.)

I brought you some flowers.

SUSIE. I saw them.

PHIL. You like these, right?

(Picking them up.)

SUSIE. I like to watch them open, yeh.

PHIL. *(At the sink, he puts water in a blender to serve as a vase.)* The guy at the store, he says they would be very slow to open – I told him that my wife liked them slow to open, he hadda guarantee it and he did.

SUSIE. They're very nice. This is hard, Phil, this is very hard.

PHIL. I know. You're right. I'm so sorry about what I did, Susie.

SUSIE. You shouldn'ta done it.

PHIL. You gotta accept my apology – whatever else happens here, you gotta accept it.

SUSIE. It's too hard. I just ache, you know – I ache all the time – when I'm with you, it don't matter, or I'm away from you, what's the difference. I don't know. I can't take it anymore, honey.

(Rising, she grabs her suitcase.)

PHIL. C'mon.

SUSIE. You're such a jerk sometimes. You really are.

PHIL. You're right. I know that.

SUSIE. *(Collapsing into the swivel chair.)* You just drive me crazy sometimes, Phil. I can't take it anymore.

(Removing her shoes, rubbing her sore feet, dropping the shoes.)

PHIL. Don't say that.

SUSIE. But it's true. It's just true.

PHIL. I wanna turn over a new leaf.

SUSIE. Like what? You can't! People can't...they can't – even if you wanted to, you –

PHIL. No, no, I can, Susie, I can – that's one'a the things I been thinkin' about.

> (*Dragging the coffee table over near her, he sits to talk to her.*)

And what I been thinkin' is if you would point these things out to me, these stupid things that when you feel you are about to start to go crazy because I am doing them, you just bring them up right then and there – and say – "You're driving me crazy Phil!"

SUSIE. What will you do?

PHIL. I'll stop it. I'll just stop it.

SUSIE. You mean, you'll try to stop.

PHIL. No, I will. I'll stop it. Whatever it is I'm doing, I'll stop it.

SUSIE. What about the baby, Phil?

PHIL. I know, I know you want to have a baby.

SUSIE. And I just don't think you will ever, I really.

PHIL. But I do, I do, too. I've thought it over and – .

SUSIE. What have you thought over? Look at me. Look me in the eye and tell me what you've thought over.

PHIL. I don't blame you – I don't blame you that you don't believe me – I wouldn't if I was you, but you should test me. That's what I would do, if I was you – I would test me.

SUSIE. I'm leaving.

> (*Leaping up,* **SUSIE** *grabs her suitcase and, carrying the bear, starts for the door.*)

PHIL. What? No, no. Wait, wait, wait.

SUSIE. I want to leave, Phil. I hate it when you talk to me like that.

PHIL. Like what?

SUSIE. Like you are – like right now –

PHIL. Like this? Like I'm talking right now?

SUSIE. Yes. It makes me crazy.

PHIL. But what is it? What am I doing? Ain't I just talking, I feel like I'm just talking.

SUSIE. With this certain quality, this certain manner.

PHIL. Yes?

SUSIE. And it's fucked up.

PHIL. But what is it?

SUSIE. You're furious at me, Phil! Don't you even know it how furious you are at me?

PHIL. I think you're mad at me, Susie. You're the one who is mad.

SUSIE. That's right. I'm livid – I'm crazy livid – but at least I know it. You don't even know it. Because you're furious at me in some secret way –

(Coming back at him to make her point as they overlap.)

PHIL. – You should hear yourself Susie, if –

SUSIE. – Some underground, sneaky way – down inside you way, some just –

PHIL. Because you're mad at me all the time. No matter what I do.

SUSIE. I'm going. I've got to go.

(She starts off, carrying the bear and her suitcase. But he leaps to block her path.)

PHIL. I mean, I KNOW I'm mad at you – SOMEWHERE – I know it, but, "It don't matter!" is what I figure. "So what!" is what I –

SUSIE. That's all it's worth to you, huh? "SO WHAT!"

PHIL. There's more important things!

SUSIE. Like what?

PHIL. Like how I love you, Susie, like how I can't live without you.

SUSIE. Oh, god.

PHIL. It's the truth.

SUSIE. You're not gonna start that again.

> *(She wants to go but sees broken glass on the*
> *floor and realizes she is in her bare feet.)*

PHIL. It's the truth.

SUSIE. It gets us nowhere! What's all this glass doing here?
Where are my shoes?

> *(Dropping the suitcase, carrying the bear, she*
> *moves back toward the kitchen, looking for*
> *her shoes.)*

I took off my shoes somewhere and I can't find them.
Where are my shoes, Phil?

PHIL. But I wanna straighten out this other thing first –
this important thing which I do it, it drives you nuts, I
don't wanna do it anymore.

SUSIE. You're doing it right now.

PHIL. Well, I'm going to stop.

SUSIE. Where are my shoes, Phil?!!

> *(As she passes near he grabs her, moves her to*
> *the couch.)*

PHIL. Susie, please. Don't be mad at me. I missed you so
much – you're so beautiful, you're so soft, you're so
beautiful and soft, and your tits are so sweet and soft,
Susie, you know how I love –

> *(He's trying to kiss her as she struggles.)*

SUSIE. NO! So we fuck and it'll be great but so what?

> *(She breaks free toward the swivel chair, still*
> *clutching the bear.)*

PHIL. Whata you mean?

SUSIE. I mean, "SO WHAT?" Don't you hear anything I say?

PHIL. I heard you, but I don't know what it means, what
you said –

SUSIE. I want more! I want us to have a life together and
share the same things and have the same favorite

things and like the same favorite movies and vacation
spots and the same TV shows and the same people and
the –

PHIL. I want that.

SUSIE. But you hate my TV shows.

PHIL. No, no. I like that one with the funny lookin' dog and
the –

SUSIE. Oh, God, now you're lying about everything.

> *(She drops into the swivel chair.)*

This is hopeless! I want to have a family! I don't care if
it's stupid to want it. OR THE WORLD'S GOING TO
END! I don't care. I want to have a baby. I have to do it.

PHIL. I know, I know.

> *(Sitting down on the coffee table to talk to
> her.)*

SUSIE. So it's impossible then, see.

> *(She rises to leave and he rises to stop her.)*

PHIL. Why?

SUSIE. Because you don't want it. You said you didn't –
have you forgotten all about that?

> *(She sits back down.)*

PHIL. But that was before!

> *(He sits.)*

SUSIE. Before what?

PHIL. Before I thought I was gonna lose you, before I felt
how –

SUSIE. So it's me!

PHIL. What?

SUSIE. It's me you want, it's just ME – you don't want to
lose ME – you're not even thinking about the poor little
baby!

> *(Leaping up to leave.)*

PHIL. No, no, I am –

SUSIE. I want you to want a little baby, not just do it, but want it.

PHIL. I do. I want it.

SUSIE. But I want you to really want it. You don't really want it.

PHIL. I do. I do, I really want it. I do. I do.

SUSIE. You don't.

PHIL. I do.

SUSIE. You're just saying it.

PHIL. Susie. Susie. Susie!

> *(He falls on his knees and pounds his fists on the floor.)*

I'm beggin'!

SUSIE. Whatsamatter with you?

PHIL. I don't know. Don't leave me. Don't leave me. This is my soul talking, Susie, this is my soul talking, it's from inside me, it's tryin' to get out, I'll fall off the end of the world. PLEASE. I wanna have a life. I wanna have a chance. I'm beggin'. Do you want me to crawl?

SUSIE. No.

> *(She starts to retreat.)*

PHIL. I will. I don't mind. I wanna. I'll crawl.

> *(And he crawls after her.)*

SUSIE. No. STOP IT!

PHIL. I'll crawl. I'll crawl.

> *(As she retreats around the chair he follows, and then he stops.)*

Here's your shoes! I found your shoes!

> *(From behind the chair he holds them high, triumphant.)*

SUSIE. *(Collapses onto the couch.)* Oh, you're drivin' me crazy. You're drivin' me crazy – this whole thing is driving me crazy.

PHIL. Don't go.

> *(Crawling to her.)*

SUSIE. Oh, I wish I was older, I wish I was older – or you was younger.

PHIL. Do you want your shoes on you?

SUSIE. Huh?

PHIL. *(He kneels before her, putting a shoe on her foot.)* I'll put your shoes on you.

SUSIE. Oh, honey, honey don't you wish we were older or younger?

PHIL. *(Kissing her feet, her legs, her knees.)* I love your feet, Honey. I love your feet. I love your legs.

SUSIE. Oh, god, oh damnit.

PHIL. Who knows why anybody loves anybody, honey? I don't. Do you? Nobody knows.

> *(Kissing her thighs, her stomach, her neck, pulling at her clothes.)*

It's okay though. It's love, you know, that's okay. Love is okay. Love is good. Love is great, ain't it.

SUSIE. Oh, god, Phil!

> *(Taking him in her arms, moving on top of him in a kiss.)*

PHIL. Love is LOVE you know. You're my honey – you're MY honey, MY honey, MY honey, MY –

> *(**SUSIE** pulls back with a gasp, as she's trying to sit up, at the same time that she keeps holding him.)*

SUSIE. Oh, oh, I can't breathe, I can't breath– just a second. Can you wait, oh –

> *(Patting him tenderly.)*

Can you wait? I gotta catch my breath.

PHIL. Don't leave, Honey, please.

SUSIE. No, no. Just a second. What's happening to me?

PHIL. It's okay.

SUSIE. My heart is pounding and racing and running – I just wanna wait and breathe – I just wanna see things and think. I wanna look around and see things and breathe and think.

PHIL. Me, too. I wanna see things.

SUSIE. Look at the table. Oh, the table.

(As they gaze at the table.)

PHIL. Yeh.

(Their heads pivot together, looking at the swivel chair.)

SUSIE. Look at the chair.

*(**PHIL** follows her, and yet there is something transformative for him, too, a clarity, as they look to the kitchen, the flowers in the blender.)*

And the blender. Look at the flowers. Look at the roses.

PHIL. I see 'em.

SUSIE. Oh, the roses. Do you see 'em?

PHIL. I see 'em.

(Now they swivel, looking at the picture above the liquor cabinet.)

Look at the picture.

SUSIE. Look at the birdies. Do you see 'em?

PHIL. I see 'em.

SUSIE. We're both seein' 'em. We're both seein' 'em.

(She faces him, holds him.)

Janice is such a negative person – you know, I don't think she believes in love – I don't think she believes in what love is – I hated being with her, she's just so negative and hopeless and down-putting about everything, she says people are empty. Everybody's empty, she says. People are empty. Do you think people are empty, Phil?

PHIL. Empty?

SUSIE. That's what she says.

PHIL. I ain't.

SUSIE. I ain't either. I don't think people are empty.

PHIL. I sure ain't.

SUSIE. Me neither.

PHIL. I may be crazy, but I ain't empty.

SUSIE. Me neither.

PHIL. Sometimes I wish I was empty.

SUSIE. Oh, Phil...

> *(Easing off the couch, she drifts to the window.)*

I was driving the other night and coming down Laurel, and out the window there were all these houses with lights on in them, and I had the feeling that if I pulled over at one of them – it would have to be the right one, and I didn't know which one it was – the right one of all those houses with the lights on – but if I took the chance, and I knocked, they might come to the door, and maybe peep out the window to see who it was, and then open the door, and smile and say, "Hello. Where have you been?"

> *(She turns from the window and looks at* **PHIL.***)*

Do you know what I mean, Phil? Do you?

PHIL. I think I do.

SUSIE. Did you ever want to be an orphan?

PHIL. What? An orphan?

SUSIE. When I was little. I really wished I was an orphan. So I could grow up and find my real family.

PHIL. Whata you mean? You mean like the one you were in wasn't the real one where you belonged, but your real one was out somewhere in the world?

SUSIE. Yeh. Like that. And I could find 'em.

PHIL. *(Startled, he stands.)* Do you know what I just remembered? I just remembered something.

SUSIE. What?

PHIL. I think I do know what you mean. It was after my old man had left. And my mom run out on us, too.

> *(Carrying the bear, he moves toward* **SUSIE** *and the window.)*

And Angelina –

> *(Raising the bear by one arm.)*

I was like this guy – only I had to be bigger. I think I did. But maybe not. My sister Angelina – she was older and there were people who thought she was my mother. Even though she wasn't. We would talk about our mother, and pretend. Angelina would take me to the window and she would say our mom was comin' that night, or the next night, or the one after. I would sit there, starin' at the door, like a dog.

SUSIE. Wow.

> *(As* **PHIL** *stares out the window, the doo-wop song* starts, and* **SUSIE** *takes his hand.)*

C'mon, Phil. C'mon.

PHIL. Yeh. Yeh.

> *(They start for the bedroom, leaving the bear on the windowsill.)*

SUSIE. It's good we got each other.

> *(He throws his arms around her and they hug for a moment, squeezing, hanging on, and then they move again.)*

It's good, it's good.

---

*A license to produce *Those the River Keeps* does not include a performance license for any third-party or copyrighted music. Licensees should create an original composition or use music in the public domain. For further information, please see Music Use Note on page 3.

PHIL. Yeh. Yeh.

> *(They go into the bedroom. The bear sits in a narrowing pool of light as the music continues.)*
>
> *(Blackout.)*

End of Play